Caitlin Crews

—

THE BRIDE HE STOLE FOR CHRISTMAS

HARLEQUIN
PRESENTS

ISBN-13: 978-1-335-56909-7

The Bride He Stole for Christmas

Copyright © 2021 by Caitlin Crews

This edition published by arrangement with Harlequin Books S.A.

For questions and comments about the quality of this book, please contact us at CustomerService@Harlequin.com.

Harlequin Enterprises ULC
22 Adelaide St. West, 40th Floor
Toronto, Ontario M5H 4E3, Canada
www.Harlequin.com

Printed in U.S.A.

"What can you possibly be thinking?" Timoney demanded, hardly able to hear her own voice over the clamor inside her, all of it spiraling around and around, blooming into sheer desire between her legs.

"The time for thinking is over, little one," Crete told her, and if anything, his stride lengthened. "Now it is time for action."

"This is an abduction! You are *kidnapping* me!"

And this time, the hand on her backside smoothed over her curves, just enough to make every nerve inside her seem to dance itself awake.

Then shudder, like she was on the very edge of shattering.

"It is," Crete agreed, all dark male satisfaction. As if he knew. "You can thank me later."

USA TODAY bestselling, RITA® Award–nominated and critically acclaimed author **Caitlin Crews** has written more than one hundred books and counting. She has a master's and PhD in English literature, thinks everyone should read more category romance and is always available to discuss her beloved alpha heroes. Just ask. She lives in the Pacific Northwest with her comic book artist husband, is always planning her next trip and will never, ever, read all the books in her to-be-read pile. Thank goodness.

Books by Caitlin Crews

Harlequin Presents

Chosen for His Desert Throne
The Sicilian's Forgotten Wife

Once Upon a Temptation

Claimed in the Italian's Castle

Royal Christmas Weddings

Christmas in the King's Bed
His Scandalous Christmas Princess

Rich, Ruthless & Greek

The Secret That Can't Be Hidden
Her Deal with the Greek Devil

Visit the Author Profile page
at Harlequin.com for more titles.

THE BRIDE HE STOLE
FOR CHRISTMAS

CHAPTER ONE

HAD TIMONEY GEORGE not felt dead inside, she might almost have enjoyed this lavish dinner the night before her farce of a wedding.

Almost.

It was merry enough, as suited a pre-wedding gathering on Christmas Eve. The guests were well-heeled and far too well-bred to speak directly of the many unfortunate undercurrents flowing up from the old stones all around them. The groom was well-liked in this particular circle, having considered himself a scion thereof for many decades. Two of his previous wives had been great favorites here as each had been part and parcel of this same crowd, as likely to claim power in Whitehall and international stock exchanges as in the titles so many had inherited.

Everything tonight was the height of sophistication, in deference to both her uncle's self-regard and his bottomless ambition. To say nothing of the groom's.

Too bad about the tart of a bride, Timoney thought from her position at her uncle's right, with a glimmer of her former wry humor.

But she locked it away. Because she didn't feel things anymore. She'd already had her fill.

Timoney looked around the hall instead. Her childhood home, entailed away to her uncle after her father's death, was done up like a stately Christmas card. Aunt Hermione was renowned for her joylessness in all things, which Timoney suspected was directly related to her endless pursuit of the skeletal figure she liked to coldly tell her rather softer and rounder teen daughters was the height of elegance. True enough, as collarbones like hers essentially acted as clothes hangers for couture. And yet despite the iron self-control and what had to be a lifetime of gnawing hunger, the woman was possessed of an excellent eye for decoration.

If Timoney had been of a more poetic

bent, she might have indulged herself with imagining that tricking out the old family hall was how Hermione expressed herself in ways otherwise unavailable to her as the thin-lipped, thinner-hipped, and much younger wife of Timoney's loathsome uncle Oliver.

But poetry was far too emotional. Aunt Hermione was likely good at decorating because she was, herself, a decoration. And like all the other trophy wives here tonight, her true vocation was in making her husband happy—likely so he'd go off and be happy elsewhere and leave her to her poinsettias and evergreen boughs.

You would do well to learn a little something from Hermione, Timoney told herself, bracingly. After all, she was staring down a future as a trophy herself.

Though a rather tarnished one, as her uncle never hesitated to remind her.

She slid her gaze toward her groom and was pleased to find that even tonight, one more sleepless night before the wedding, she felt the same wealth of nothing she'd felt since her uncle had announced that Timoney's choices were stark. Either marry his business associate, Julian Browning-Case, or be cut off from the family forever.

It wasn't that Timoney liked her extended family all that much that the loss of them would be devastating in any way. But after losing her parents—and afterward, losing what was left of her heart so wholly and irrevocably—she didn't have it in her to walk away from what she had left. She also knew that her parents would have hated it if she had. They had always told her that Oliver might have faults, but it was better to believe that he was doing the best he could.

Timoney had seen no evidence of that. But really, it was the least she could do after her scandalous behavior had, according to her uncle, blackened the family name forever.

She was well aware that her uncle's real concern had nothing to do with the family's reputation. It was her reputation, not the family's, and why would anyone care what the orphaned daughter of the former heir got up to? The Georges had old money and unlike some, had held on to it. And every family with a drop of noble blood in England had at least one embarrassing member.

Especially among the younger generations, who tended to perform for the pages of *Tatler*—especially if it horrified their parents. It was an excuse for her uncle to flex his power as the head of the family, that was all.

But none of that mattered any longer. Julian Browning-Case, while not what Timoney would describe as *doting* in any way, was not openly vicious. He was three times her age, had not insulted her even when her uncle did, and was shaped like a man who could look forward to future heart trouble. To that end, the kindest advice her aunt had ever given her—moments before entering the engagement party a month ago that Timoney had worked to pretend wasn't happening as it did—was a pointed reminder that the Browning-Cases were not known for being particularly long-lived.

Hermione had seen Timoney balk, just outside the doors of the hall. And because Oliver had not, it had likely felt safe for her to lean in and offer a dollop of her own brand of wisdom.

For those of us who make practical instead of romantic marriages, Hermione had

said with a curious expression on her face—
as if, Timoney had reflected from the usual
distance from which she observed anything
these days, seeing her niece for the very first
time. *Perspective is everything. One must
always weigh one's—ah—expected future
solitude against the manifold joys of one's
actual marriage while it exists in its current
form. It is a delicate math.*

That was the closest Hermione had ever
come to any kind of surrogate maternal expression. That, too, was just as well.

Because Timoney did not wish to think
too much about her parents—or her actual,
horribly missed mother. It was too hard. Too
painful, though it was nearly three years ago
now. The two of them had been gone so
quickly, so suddenly. And then everything
had changed so rapidly. One terrible, irrevocable event after another so that Timoney
rather thought that if she had the capacity to
feel anything inside any longer, anything at
all, a night like this might have wrecked her.

For surely it ought to be painful to be
back here in this house where she had once
been so happy. When joy had been at the
heart of everything, waiting around every

corner, filling all of these ancient rooms. Some of her fondest memories were of running through these halls that had seemed far lighter then, lit up with her parents' love for each other. And their boundless delight in her.

She had been on the verge of her twentieth birthday when she'd gotten the call that an icy road on a cold March evening had taken away the two people dearest to her. Mere miles from this old manor house, hidden away in hedges and stone.

Uncle Oliver had wasted no time. As the new head of the family, he was in charge of the George fortune—and Timoney's trust—until her twenty-eighth birthday. But he hadn't wished to trouble himself with paying for her until then. He had yanked her out of her beloved finishing school in the French Alps two weeks after her parents' funeral. Once she'd come back to the house he'd already claimed as his, he had informed her that for the next eight years she was to do as he bid her because, as far as he was concerned, she was a charity case. And it was too bad for Timoney that he was no fan of charity.

Even then, he had offered her choices, such as they were. She was to marry to suit him—because she would be a useless drain on him for nearly a decade aside from her ability to please his rich friends and access their wealth and favor—or she was welcome to make her own way in the world.

Timoney wet her lips with the wine on the table before her, an easy way to check to make sure her mouth was in the polite near-smile shape that was expected of her. And she nodded along, pretending to listen as the swell of conversation went on all around her.

Something in her shifted, almost unpleasantly, as she thought of the girl she'd been back then. Puffed up with outrage and grief. Filled with a deep loathing of her evil uncle and appalled at his demands. Did he really think he could treat her like a *chattel*? She was newly twenty then, and modern—not a medieval twelve.

She'd told him where he could go, she'd swanned off to London, and she'd taken the first job she could find. It turned out she was an excellent fit to do a bit of PR for a corporation she'd never heard of and didn't care to learn much about. But that was the benefit of her brand of public relations. Timoney didn't need to move the product—she threw the parties. She already had the kind of connections businessmen in suits were always gasping to exploit, so it mattered little that she knew nothing at all about the things they got up to in their endless meetings. All that mattered was that she was blonde and could get certain names to turn up, which guaranteed press.

And for a good eighteen months she'd had a lovely time. She'd shared a flat in Central London—it was more a house, really, but they all called it a flat because that felt more career-girls-in-the-Smoke—with a few girls she knew from school. All of them had been in the same sort of purgatory, cast out into the world by the heads of their families with vague expectations that they should prove they weren't entirely useless—even though everyone knew that in five years or ten or so the trust funds would start kicking in and all the proof would be pointless. They'd all been playing the same sort of waiting game in those years, trading this party for that in all the trendiest corners of giddy London, all of them counting down the days until they could stop pretending.

It would be better, Timoney had often thought back then, not to know that there was a future, fixed date upon which one would never have to worry about paying a bill again. Especially when she couldn't go beg Daddy to do it for her like her friends.

Then she'd met Crete Asgar and she'd stopped thinking of any future that didn't involve him.

Even thinking his name here, now, at a table filled with the kind of braying toffs he disdained, made her fight back a deep shiver.

There was a straight line between that fateful night and this one. It had all been headed for disaster from the start—though she hadn't known that then. She hadn't known, or wanted to know, a thing but Crete.

And Timoney was pleased that her heart had been ripped out and trampled, because it no longer beat too hard. It no longer threatened to burst. She could stand here, on the night before her wedding to another man she hardly knew, and congratulate herself on feeling very little at all.

Because after a whirlwind six months as Crete's mistress, he had finished with her two months ago. Brutally.

She felt proud that she could think of it that way. Such a quiet little sentence. *He had finished with her.* Such bloodless words to describe that scene in that penthouse of his, all modern angles and cold lines set up there above the Thames, where he'd taken everything that Timoney was, shredded it, then set it all on fire.

It's better this way, she assured herself. *There's nothing left to worry about losing.*

She heard her uncle's voice from beside her and snapped back into the here and now, at this holiday dinner party that was supposedly in her honor.

"I hope you aren't lapsing off into any unfortunate second thoughts," Uncle Oliver said coldly at her elbow. Timoney had no memory of the rest of the party rising from the banquet table, but they must have done. For now she could see straight across to her favorite tapestry on the far wall, though staring about the brightly lit, festive room didn't warm her as it might have once. It could have been ash for all she cared.

Maybe it was.

"I don't have thoughts, Uncle," she replied coolly. "Second or otherwise. You have forbidden it."

His hand was on her elbow then, and he squeezed far too hard, but she did not give him the satisfaction of wincing. No, indeed. She felt the pain of it, and some part of it thrilled her. That she could feel even a sensation like that, her uncle's brand of quietly sadistic violence, and react not at all.

"Julian tells me that you declined his offer of a drink last night," her uncle hissed into her ear. "I thought we were agreed on our course of action." Meaning he'd ordered her to offer the groom a preview of what he was purchasing.

"I will be marrying Julian soon enough," Timoney said, turning her gaze toward her uncle. And maybe it wasn't entirely true to say she felt nothing. Only that she showed nothing. Because, she could admit, she took no little pleasure in the way she gazed dispassionately at this man whose distaste for her seemed to bounce off her now. Like rubber. She especially liked that it clearly enraged him. "So no reason to rush into it."

"What sudden preciousness is this?" her uncle snarled. He leaned in closer, across the corner of the table they shared. "You're damaged goods, Timoney. That cretin's fingerprints are all over you. You flaunted yourself on his arm and he made no secret of the base physicality of your union in every photograph taken by the baying press. Yet you dare pull on a cloak of false modesty?"

Timoney pointedly tugged her elbow out of his grasp. "It's not modesty, Uncle. It's strategy. Why give myself away for free with the wedding so soon? What if he was disappointed?" She shrugged as if they were discussing livestock. Well. She supposed they were. "Damaged goods or not, why would a man pay full price for something when he'd already had it at a discount?"

If she wasn't already ruined—and not in the way her uncle imagined—this would destroy her, she was sure. This cold, dispassionate discussion of the marital rights she'd be expected to perform tomorrow.

Said marital rights that were, she was well aware, something her elderly husband was eagerly awaiting. Julian had made his interest in her clear since the moment he'd laid eyes on her here at one of her uncle's dreadful soirees not long after she'd slunk back to the ancestral pile in shame, still licking her wounds.

Though it was more accurate to say that she wasn't so much *licking wounds* as she was attempting to…pretend that she was still a person. Instead of the tiny little pile of crushed-out cinders that Crete had left behind him that night.

It had taken her uncle only a few weeks to talk her into this marriage that benefited him the most. He had ranted on about the shame she'd brought on the family. About the stain of it that would cling to his own three daughters if Timoney was allowed to continue her downward spiral.

By his reckoning, having been sullied and discarded by the likes of Crete Asgar—as infamous for his entirely self-made wealth as for his contempt of the sort of hereditary riches that Oliver now possessed—Timoney was no better than the sorts of addicts one could find cluttering up the streets. Oliver did not view such addictions as diseases.

They were choices, he liked to declare. For it was one thing to genteelly pop painkillers like all the women in Oliver's circles did to survive their practical marriages. It was something else again to allow one's weaknesses to be so *visible*, and Timoney was already on the wrong side of that equation.

For she had appeared in too many papers Oliver's friends actually read, clearly in thrall to her unacceptable lover.

What next? he had thundered at a family dinner a week or so after she'd returned. Would she turn to modeling—which, in his mind, was merely prostitution by another name.

I will take that as a compliment, Uncle, Timoney had replied over her chilled soup with a flash of her former defiance. *I had no idea you rated my looks so highly.*

That had gotten her a slap.

More than that, it had gotten her uncle thinking about how best he could use her looks to his advantage.

You're the spitting image of your mother, he had said not long after. Timoney knew this was true, and it was one more thing painful for her to try not to think about. She grew more like her mother every day. The blond hair, the wide smile, the pointed chin. So similar, and yet Crete had seen to it that there was nothing resembling the spark of joy in her that had always brightened her mother's gaze.

It was better not to think of such things. It only made her sad.

Beside her, her uncle seemed to still be turning over the notion that Timoney might actually have acted strategically in his interest. But she knew it wouldn't last. She had only to inhale too loudly to agitate him anew.

"On that note," she said now, "I believe I will call it a night. I expect tomorrow will be long." And arduous in more ways than one.

"You and Julian will be staying in his guest suite tomorrow night," her uncle told her coldly. "He does not wish to travel after the reception. And I had better not hear of any impediment to a swift and comprehensive consummation of your union."

"What a pity we can't gather everyone round for viewing of the marital sheets," Timoney said drily.

Uncle Oliver's gaze was scathing. "To what end? That is a ceremony for virgins. I think we both know that there is not an unspoiled inch on your body, girl. Not after letting that animal rut all over you."

Timoney couldn't keep herself from thinking about the way he'd said that as she left her own party, smiling distantly at the assembled guests, all of them cold like Aunt Hermione, cruel like her uncle, or simply self-satisfied like her husband-to-be. They would go on, no doubt toasting their own wealth and consequence, well into the wee hours.

Maybe there would be so much toasting it would stave off the worst of any *comprehensive consummating.*

"Tomorrow, my dear," said Julian when she crossed his path, his creased and reddened face perhaps a shade too jolly for her liking.

"Tomorrow," she agreed, and had to force the ends of her mouth to curve.

Soon enough, she told herself harshly as she took herself out of the grand hall, she would be lying beneath that man. Far more intimately acquainted with his brand of jolly than she liked. It was not a pleasant thought. It had been better in the abstract, when the wedding was *someday*, not soon. Not tomorrow.

Timoney stopped at the foot of the stairs that led up toward the bedchambers. She looked toward the banquet hall she'd just left. Then, following an urge she could hardly name, she turned and fled out into the cold gardens.

Because Timoney knew full well that she would do as women always had. Or she hoped she would. She would lie back, close her eyes, and think not of England, but of the man who had imprinted himself upon her so completely that it was not clear to her that she would ever take another breath without feeling him somehow inside her all over again.

She was glad she'd thought to grab her cloak on her way outside, for the night was cold. A mist made the winter garden mysterious, especially when the moon shone through.

It was a silent night indeed.

And if Timoney had let herself feel, all the things that moved inside her then might have taken her to her knees. Right there where the flowers would bloom again in spring, long after she had calcified and died anew inside this marriage of hers. Long after Julian carried her off to his estate, sampled her, and then added her to his collection of stodgy statuary that was often written up in guidebooks, or so he claimed.

She didn't buckle or fall over. She drew the warm cloak around her and sank down on the first stone bench she found, letting her eyes fall shut.

And she worked so hard to keep herself from thinking about Crete or that last night with him too closely. But tonight was the last time she would be able to think about him as a singular event in her life. In her body.

From tomorrow forward, Crete would be the gold standard—but there would be Julian, too. And here, in the privacy of this frozen garden, she allowed herself to take a peek at all the things she truly felt about that notion.

Shock. Despair. Horror.

And a kind of resolute acceptance, because there was no changing this.

Crete Asgar had swept into her life like a wildfire, burned her to a crisp, then had left nothing in his wake save charred ground.

She could remember each and every moment with such distinct and spectacular detail it was like punishing herself. Every touch of his hand. The first, life-altering curve of his hard mouth. The kiss that had knocked her sideways and stolen her heart.

She had given him her innocence and in return, he had taken her apart.

He had made her body feel and do things she had not believed could be real. She still woke in the night, her body electric and alive, her heart pounding so hard it hurt and his taste in her mouth.

Sometimes she would dream that she was still living with him, the heat of his possession making the whole of that penthouse glow, all its hard angles and edges softened by the fire in the way he looked at her. The way he held her. And how all-encompassing it was between them.

You are a terrible distraction, he had told her once and, foolish girl that she was, she had thought of that as a compliment.

To be able to distract a man of his singular focus. A man who had established himself with his single-mindedness. A man who had been flung out of his father's family the moment he was of age and left to fend for himself—because he was a bastard, evidence of an affair, and soundly unwanted.

Crete Asgar had not cared who wanted him. What he wanted was power.

It had taken him five years to make his first fortune. And then he had made so many subsequent fortunes that it had become something of an international sport to guess his net worth.

She should have known better than to imagine a man like that would ever welcome too many distractions.

Timoney stayed there on her cold bench, her eyes screwed shut as her heart began pounding again.

If she let herself, she could almost imagine that the Christmas Eve air was thick with the tension that had always hummed between the two of them. Only between them, and obvious from the start. She had looked up from her mobile, there outside a club in London so trendy it had already disappeared before that weekend had ended, checking in big names to another party. She couldn't remember the supposed purpose of that particular evening.

What she could remember in stark detail was lifting up her gaze from the screen of her mobile when she'd sensed the man standing before her.

She could remember her first sight of him so clearly. His dark black hair. The gleaming arrogance of his shocking blue gaze. He was tall and perfectly built, though she spent her life around men who could claim the same. Yet there was something about Crete Asgar. He was bolder. Wilder. It was as if he carried a storm with him, and it was evident in the width of his shoulders, the hard planes of his face. He was a perfect combination of his Greek mother and Scandinavian father, and it was easy to imagine him as some kind of Spartan warrior, prepared to storm the gates of Valhalla if he wished.

Looking at him had felt like an ancient ritual, sparked with drums deep within her and ecstatic dancing beneath the hidden moon. Timoney had felt as if the act of locking gazes with him was something like…obscene. Too precious and private to be happening out on a London street.

She'd seen a pulse beat in his neck. She'd seen a kind of recognition flaring his gaze.

He'd reached out his hand to slide it over her jaw, as if to test whether she was real, and she'd been lost.

It was possible she had never been found.

Crete had muttered a curse. He'd taken her hand, then led her away from her post and into the party.

She remembered the heaving club as if it was a part of him, of them, of that mad current that had flared between them from the start. She had felt it between her legs. She'd felt it all over her skin, like a terrible tattoo.

Terrible and wonderful, and then he had drawn her behind him into what she realized, only much later, was a cloakroom.

Who are you? he'd asked, breathing her in, and then his mouth had been upon her.

She liked to think that she had found herself again at the stamp of his hard possession, the slide of his tongue against hers.

Crete had not so much kissed her as taken her, stormed her, claimed her forever.

And later, she would learn the details that made what happened there marginally less sordid—not that she had cared at the time. That his security detail had paid off the cloakroom worker and stood sentry at the

door, so there was no possibility that anyone would walk in on them.

But Timoney hadn't known that then. She
had only been swept away. The fire between
them so intense, so overwhelming, that her
only choice had not been whether or not to
surrender, but only how. Or how much.

She told herself to recast the scene in her
mind, now, all these bitter months later. She
told herself it had been a sickness on her
part that had led her to tear her mouth from
his to follow a spark of feminine intuition
she couldn't possibly have named when she
had so little experience to her name. Still,
she'd sunk down onto her knees before him,
because she'd wanted nothing more than to
worship at the altar of… Whatever this was.
Whatever he was.

Whoever he was.

She'd never done such a thing in her life.
She had never *wanted* to do such a thing,
but her hands had seemed to find the fly of
his trousers of their own accord. Timoney
had wrenched the zipper down, finding him
huge and hot and pushing out to meet her.

And then she taught herself what it was
to worship a man, there on her knees with

the music lighting her up, the drums deep within, and a need so profound it made her sway her hips back and forth as she knelt there and took him deep into her mouth.

She followed instincts she hadn't known she possessed, running her tongue up the length of him, then sucking him deep. Out here in a cold Christmas Eve, she told herself she should be ashamed. That she should feel wretched that she had esteemed herself so little, that she had debased herself like that, losing herself completely in the slide and the stretch of him inside her mouth.

But try as she might, that wasn't how she remembered it.

It was never how she remembered it.

For Timoney had never felt so alive, so powerful. She knew his strength by the way his hands gripped her hair, taking control of her, guiding her head, and then, as everything seemed to brighten, to get bolder, to crystallize into something—

He had pulled her away and stared down the length of his body, his chest moving and his face so intense with need and hunger that he had seemed nearly cruel.

But the kind of cruelty she wanted to wrap herself around and writhe against.

Have you ever done this before?

It had been a low, rough whisper.

And it had felt like a sacrament as she'd knelt and beheld him. A quiet, sacred moment, all theirs.

Timoney had been lying to her friends for years, pretending she possessed the casualness and sophistication they all seemed to exude so effortlessly. They had assumed she had partaken of the same experiences they did, and she had never corrected that impression. But she couldn't lie to the stranger. To him.

She had shaken her head, *no.*

And an expression she could not possibly have read had flickered across the carved sculpture of his face.

He had tucked himself away, wincing slightly, and had pulled her to her feet.

Have you ever done any of this before? he had asked.

She'd shaken her head again.

Tell me, he had ordered her. *Tell me what you've done.*

Nothing, she had confessed. *I've only been*

kissed once before, and not like that. And you're the only man I ever...

Her voice had betrayed her, but she would have betrayed herself a thousand times again for the look on his face then.

So possessive. So deeply male it hurt.

Tell me your name, he had ordered her. *And then tell me what it will take to make you mine.*

She shuddered at that, here on her frigid bench on this lonely Christmas Eve, her body as alive and greedy as she had been that night.

And Timoney wanted to scream out all the anguish, all the artless fury that he'd left her with. His betrayal so absolute that it had taken her whole months to fully comprehend exactly what he'd done. Chucked her out. Forgotten her name. Washed his hands of her completely.

Yet tonight, when she should have been reveling in exactly how cold and dead inside she'd become, it was as if he was here. A ghostly presence in the mist, and it seemed deeply unfair that any ghost could fill a cold garden the way he had always overwhelmed a room.

She blew out a breath and told herself not to be such a fool. For once.

Crete was immovable. A terrible wall of stone and silence, and some part of her had known that from the start.

And still she had run straight for all that brick and smashed herself apart.

"Have you fallen asleep, Timoney?" came the terrible, wonderful, familiar voice.

Timoney wrenched open her eyes, and as she did, the moon came out from behind the clouds.

And it was impossible, but Crete was there. He stood before her looking beautiful and dangerous, as ever. He was sheer male glory in his typical uniform, one of those dark, bespoke suits that made love to his body in all the ways she longed to do.

It was not possible, and yet every hair on her body seemed to stand on end, so she knew that it was real. That this was no dream.

That somehow, Crete Asgar was stood in the remains of the garden while her uncle and her husband-to-be carried on toasting the wedding up in the manor house.

"Crete…" she whispered.

And all the feelings she'd been holding at bay slammed back into her, and worse, were lit up with hope.

Because he had finished with her because she'd committed the cardinal sin of telling him she loved him. Why would he be here, on the night before her wedding no less, unless he was finally ready to admit what she had always suspected, that he loved her, too? What else could bring him out on Christmas Eve?

"You can't possibly marry that old man in the morning," he told her, and he did not sound like a man tortured by love. He did not sound tortured at all. Or in love. If anything, Crete sounded impatient. "I have standards, Timoney. Obviously any lover after me will be a downgrade. But this verges on an insult."

CHAPTER TWO

CRETE ASGAR DID not chase women before he went to bed with them.

He certainly did not chase them afterward.

There was absolutely no reason he should have found himself in a frozen garden on Christmas Eve, no matter who his former mistress was marrying.

It was a matter of no little astonishment that he was even aware of Timoney's betrothal. He supposed it was possible that all of the women he had once claimed as his for a time had moved on into matrimony, but it was of no matter to him, as he could barely recall any of them.

And yet he felt as if he'd been assaulted by Timoney's engagement from the start. All the tabloids that had taken such delight in chasing the two of them all over London while they were together had taken an equal delight in arch commentary regarding Timoney's new choice of man. He hadn't gone looking for these accounts—and yet, it had seemed as if he could not avoid them.

Crete was not normally one to heed or even notice the opinions of others, so he had dismissed each and every article that had flashed at him from newsstands. For the whole month since her engagement announcement—a mere two months since the end of his relationship with her, not that he had counted—he had tended to his usual business affairs and told himself it was no matter to him what his former lover did.

He told himself this repeatedly, because it was usually true. If she chose to shackle herself to some old man, what was it to him?

As it turned out, Crete cared a great deal.

Far more than he would have liked.

And yet, having never chased a woman in his life, he had found himself...at something of a loss. Or as close to as he was capable of coming to such a state, given that he did not lose. As a matter of preference, will, and precedent.

He had never visited Timoney's family home. Having been ejected from what passed for his own family twice—first as a toddler and then again when he was a young man—Crete had never found himself particularly interested in the familial institution. He had made his fortune with no help from anyone and disdained these English notions of blood and honor as a matter of course. He also could not recall Timoney ever speaking too much about the people she came from— but then, they had never done much in the way of talking.

But it had still been easy enough to find his way to this rambling estate in the quiet of the countryside, far enough outside town that London seemed like it belonged in a different lifetime altogether. That was the thing with these English landowners. The houses themselves had names and everyone knew how to find them.

When he'd set out from London tonight, Crete had told himself he was only going for a drive. Then, as he found that he was inexorably winding his way into Oxfordshire, he told himself that he would stop by to see her, that was all. Have a lovely cup of tea, the English answer to any awkward moment, and be on his way again.

That it was Christmas Eve hadn't really occurred to him. But if it had, it wouldn't have stopped him. He had about as much use for Christmas as he did for families.

The real question was why he thought it necessary that he see her at all.

For Crete never returned to scenes of crimes, passion, or pain. Ever. He did not look back, for his life was about new horizons. He had always had a terrible hunger that he preferred to slake as often as possible, which was why he kept mistresses. He liked his sex consistent, constant, and without all the games involved in meeting a new woman. And when they claimed they'd fallen in love with him, as they often did when they sensed his interest was waning, he simply moved on.

Though another truth was that after separating from Timoney, Crete had found his typical hunger…changed. Not muted or removed, but somehow, though two months had passed, he had not yet slaked his thirst.

And he had told himself a hundred stories to explain that bizarre lapse in his usual habits, but the truth was before him now.

Timoney, with her hair like spun gold flowing down her back tonight, catching the moonlight and gleaming brighter. Timoney, wrapped in a cloak that looked thick against the cold night air, but did nothing to disguise the lush ripeness of her figure. Perhaps it was that he recalled it too well.

And maybe it was the Greek in him who could never get enough of her eyes, as blue as the Mediterranean, even in the shadows of this cold winter garden.

"What are you doing here?" she asked him, staring up at him as if he was a ghost.

It was possible that Crete had entertained the notion that merely glancing upon him would wake her up from whatever spell she was laboring under. It was possible that he'd expected her to fly into his arms, the way she always had while they were together.

He scowled when she did not. "Surely that should be obvious."

She did not look chastened. Her blue eyes blazed. Her chin tilted upward. "I can think of no reason."

Something sparked in him, and it surprised him. For she was as beautiful as ever, that was true. And God knew, he was a man who not only appreciated beautiful things, but had appreciated her beauty in particular. Moreover, there were certain brands of fire that she'd shared with him and he had greatly enjoyed the flames of each.

But this was different.

Because for once, Timoney was not looking at him with her customary awe and emotion.

In fact, to his astonishment, she appeared to be glaring at him. At *him*.

With what he could only call hostility.

He would not say he was *disconcerted*, per se. But only because he did not get disconcerted. His scowl deepened. "I was in the neighborhood."

"Crete Asgar himself? Roaming about England's greenest hills? Surely not." He was sure he had to be mistaken, but she sounded…mocking. Sharply amused, when he could see no call for amusement. "You were always at pains to tell me that the countryside held no allure for you. What could a man who owns his own Mediterranean islands want with rainy hedgerows and stodgy Georgian facades?"

"And yet here I am. In the neighborhood. As you see."

Crete had the strangest sensation then, when all she did was gaze back at him. And not as if she was transported by his glory as in simpler times. He could not even name the sensation, it was so foreign. And then, as she made no move toward him, he belatedly understood. He had never seen her look at him like this before.

As if she did not want him.

As if she did not want him, which was impossible.

It was unthinkable.

"You must know that I'm getting married in the morning," was what she said. Eventually. In a tone he did not like. "Have you come to wish me well? Perhaps you needed my registry details?"

Crete took that in, aware that a different kind of heat was humming in him. His months with Timoney had been lush. Sweet. From their explosive first moments in that ridiculous club straight through to the inevitable finish. He sometimes thought that had she not so foolishly fallen in love with him, they might still be together—though he very rarely kept a mistress for more than a few months. She had been that delectable.

What she had never been was sardonic.

He couldn't deny that it surprised him. But it also made him hard, so there was that.

Crete had deeply appreciated her sweetness. Yet deep down, he was a man who appreciated a fight. It was hard not to appreciate the only thing he had ever known.

"Did you grow a backbone, little one?" he asked quietly, letting the hunger and the need wash over him. Through him, like a baptism, out in the dark and cold with the mist and the moon and no more stories to explain the truth away. He wanted her. "I think perhaps it suits you."

"Maybe it's a backbone." But she sniffed. "Or maybe it's that I'm wearing another man's ring. Either way, there's nothing here for you, Crete. You made that clear."

She had not fought with him that night. That was what he had found himself brooding over in the days, the weeks, the two long months since. She had cried out her love. He had shared his philosophy with her and then, to prevent any misunderstandings, he had ordered her to go.

Standard practice, really.

Normally, the kind of women who dared tell him that they loved him were outraged at that point. They would scream at him, berate him, prove to him beyond any shadow of a doubt that their love was more squarely focused on his bank details than anything else.

But Timoney had only stared at him, tears rolling down her perfect cheeks, her soft lips parted as if she found it hard to breathe.

He hated to admit how many times that image had distracted him as he went about his business.

And now she was sitting there on the little bench before him, staring up at him like he was a stranger. He couldn't bear it. So he reached out to fit his palm to her cheek as he had a thousand times before—

But unlike before, she knocked his hand away.

And then surged to her feet. "You don't get to show up here in the middle of the night and just…touch me whenever you feel like it."

"Do you not wish for me to touch you?"

He let his hand fall back to his side. "I think you are a liar, Timoney."

"If you wished to touch me, you shouldn't have tossed me aside like so much trash," she threw back at him. "Should you?"

"It wasn't the touching I had an issue with."

He thought she might shout at him, and he couldn't decide if he would find that exciting—or if it would once again make her seem like a stranger to him.

But she didn't.

Her chest was rising and falling rapidly, the cloak spilling out all around her, a deep red. She put him in mind of some kind of fairy tale, out here in the misty moonlight, when he had as little use for children's stories as he did for Christmas Eve.

Crete was not one for holidays in general, but especially not this holiday. It seemed a part and parcel of that kind of home and hearth, overtly familial notion he had never really experienced. But Timoney in a red cloak had him feeling the closest to festive he'd felt in a long time.

Maybe ever.

"Why are you here, Crete?" she asked, her voice even. When the Timoney he knew had never seemed to have herself in control. She'd never indicated she wanted to try to keep herself in control. "You made it clear to me that you don't care about me. Crystal clear. So why should it matter to you who I marry?"

He let out a bark of disbelief. "You cannot marry this man. To begin with, he is ancient."

"Some would say he must be filled with wisdom, then." Her smile seemed sharp. "What luck."

"He cannot possibly satisfy you, Timoney." Crete studied her. "I could barely keep up with you."

There was a telltale bloom of color in her cheeks, but all she did was square her shoulders. "That remains to be seen. My previous experience left much to be desired."

He laughed. "We both know that is a lie."

"Yes, Crete. We had chemistry. But I can't say I have much admiration for the way it ended." She crossed her arms before her, as if she was warding him off. And she frowned at him. At *him*. "And here's what I know about Julian. He will not leave me. He will not cruelly cast me aside if I say the wrong thing. He will honor the promises he makes me tomorrow. Any way I look at it, marrying him seems like a good bargain."

"You cannot be serious."

Crete moved closer to her. And he, who prided himself on his iron self-control to match his will of steel, had no idea how his hands rose to grip her slender shoulders. Only that they did, and that holding her made him…feel.

He concentrated on the part he understood. The heat. And the faint scent of her, teasing him on the cold breeze like a memory.

"Let me assure you of something," she whispered, her chin still high and her arms still crossed. "Unlike some people standing in this garden, I do not take relationships lightly. But I certainly do not take the prospect of marriage lightly, either. You can be certain that whatever else I might be in regard to my wedding tomorrow, I am deadly serious."

Crete zeroed in on the most egregious part of that little speech. "You think I took our relationship lightly?"

She scowled at him, another first. Then she lifted her hands as if to knock his grip off her shoulders. But instead, her fingers braceleted his wrists, not quite managing to close, and stayed there.

And he had the notion that she could feel the way his blood pumped in his veins. That she could feel it in her, too. That their bodies were still that connected, that attuned.

The song of it seemed to pool in his sex, then beat hard, like a drum.

"The only thing you take seriously is your money," she threw at him.

And she clearly meant it to wound.

But Crete only laughed and pulled her closer, because he could smell that wildflower honey scent of her everywhere. And he could feel the heat of that in his blood, too, because everything about Timoney was heat and honey, longing and that need so deep, it felt like it was in his bones.

"Yes, I care about my money," he confessed. He laughed again. "I think you'll find it comes as a habit to those who remember having none." He jerked his chin at the sprawling mansion behind her and the extensive grounds. It had been a ten-minute drive in from the lane to find the house. "Not all of us grew up surrounded by such finery."

"I think you'll find that the rags-to-riches tale is more relatable after your first fortune," Timoney retorted. "Not so much your tenth. Or is it your twentieth by now?" Her eyes were bright with a new kind of fire, and it took him long moments to understand that it was temper. Why did he want to drown himself in her—temper and all? "I have all of seventy pounds to my name at present, Crete. Tell me which one of us is privileged?"

"Seventy pounds, a rich fiancé, and a fortune to come." He shook his head at her. "You're not exactly the Little Match Girl yourself, are you?"

"What I am or am not is none of your concern," she threw at him. "You still haven't told me what you're doing here. Did you pop round to infuriate me?"

"That is but a happy side effect."

"I would have thought you'd be thrilled to find that I was getting married." Her eyes flashed. "No need to worry about scraping me off your boot heel if I'm someone else's problem, isn't that right?"

He didn't think he'd said precisely that to her, though Crete knew that it aligned perhaps too closely with his feelings on the topic. For it was a fact that he had always been delighted when—if—he heard that his former mistresses had moved on. There was far less chance that they would hang about making things tedious that way.

But this was Timoney.

And nothing about her was tedious.

And he was *here*, wasn't he? It spoke volumes.

"Very well," she was saying, in that bristling British way. "I can see that you really did come here just to be difficult."

"Some would argue that I do this without even trying."

"Here's the great news, Crete," she said, and he felt certain that he would not find whatever news she was about to share at all great. "When I was your mistress, it fell to me to try to keep you happy. And I failed at that. I failed at it so completely that you not only finished things, but ordered me to move out immediately—then made sure your security detail saw to it that I did."

"That is not entirely true." But it was close enough to make him uncomfortable, he was forced to acknowledge.

"Whatever it is you want tonight, both you and I already know that I don't have what it takes to please you," Timoney said. Not as if she was apologizing or even particularly broken up about it. She inclined her head. "So perhaps you'd best move along."

It was an order, clearly. But against his will, all he could think about was all the ways she really had made him happy.

Again and again and again.

He had moved her into his flat within a week of meeting her—and with only the most superficial vetting—because once he'd tasted her, he couldn't bear to have a single free moment and not indulge himself with more of her. His craving for her had been so intense that he'd reasoned the only way to handle it was to immerse himself.

Completely.

And still it hadn't been enough.

For the first time, he admitted that maybe,

just maybe, there had been some small part of him that had been relieved when she'd crossed his uncrossable line that night. When she'd spilled over with those words she should never have said.

Especially when he was not the least bit tired with her yet.

Because he had spent whole months consumed with her, and maybe, just maybe, he had been grateful to get his head back.

But he realized now, as the mist swirled around between them and her blue eyes glistened in the dark, that he'd only been fooling himself.

"You cannot marry that man," he growled at her.

"Why not?" she tossed back at him. "It seems to me that Julian is as good as anyone else. Better than most."

"He is neither. He is a cretinous gasbag who sheds wives—"

"The way you shed mistresses?"

He didn't care for that. "There are no similarities between us."

"That's why I agreed to marry him in the first place," she snapped. "I understand his expectations of me, Crete. There's no pretense."

"Your body. Your soul. Your life."

Timoney laughed at that, but the sound was bitter, and he hated that. She had been so joyful. So bright. He hated that he had rendered her something less than that. That he had taken it along with her innocence.

Maybe he truly was the monster his father's wife had always maintained he was.

All evidence suggested it.

"Imagine that," Timoney said when she stopped laughing, and her blue eyes shone cold. "Julian wants the same things from me that you did. But look at all he's willing to offer me in return. His name. Children, if I wish it. Primarily my body, yes, but the difference between the two of you is that he's not afraid to sweeten the pot. Nor will he cast me aside if I displease him, unlike his former wives. Divorce would be far too expensive. My uncle has seen to it."

That she was comparing him to the likes of Julian Browning-Case was insult enough. That he was losing by her reckoning was insupportable.

"You cannot marry him," Crete said again, while a terrible storm wailed in him as he pictured, against his will, what she was describing. Surrendering herself. Selling herself. Giving the decrepit old man that body of hers that Crete understood, with a certain resignation, he had long since considered only and ever his.

It turned out that he was not prepared to share.

"Why not?" she demanded. Her hands turned to fists and she knocked them into his chest. "Give me one good reason why I shouldn't?"

He welcomed the faint kiss of her fists. He welcomed any touch from her at all, and what did it say that he'd fallen so far? But there was no arguing with the truth. There was only accepting it and moving forward.

Crete had built his life on exactly this premise.

And he was more than happy to provide her with all the reasons she needed to see this truth as he had. Surely that, in the end, was why he'd come here.

Surely that was what mattered.

"Because, little one," he growled at her, "you have belonged to me since the moment we met. You still do."

And then Crete proved it the way he always had, by crushing his mouth to hers.

CHAPTER THREE

TIMONEY HAD THOUGHT this would never happen again.

She'd been sure. He'd made certain she was sure.

But now he was kissing her again, as if there had been no separation. She was kissing him back as if her heart had never been crushed. And all her dreams, all her memories, faded away as the searingly beautiful reality of it took hold, sweeping through her and lighting her up as if she had never dimmed.

As if there had never been the faintest hint of darkness.

The taste of him. The heat. The way a kiss from this man was nothing so simple as the word implied. There was no fairy tale here. There was no swelling soundtrack in the distance with magic all around. It was too intense for any of that. Too wild.

Too much.

And even though Timoney knew better now, even though he had taught her too well that the abandon she felt when she was close to him was a lie—

How could any of that matter when his mouth was on hers again?

When finally—*finally*—she felt alive again?

As she always had, Timoney melted into him, and that, too, was an opportunity for more intensity. Because the wall of his chest was hard and hot, and far better than she remembered it. When she had remembered it in excruciating detail. And it was this particular stone, this wall of toned muscle, that she had tried so hard to shatter herself against, hadn't she?

And had. Over and over again.

Like every kiss, it was like the first.

Unlike so many others, Timoney knew, now, that it could also be the last.

But the mad storm of sensation washed over her and through her, and it didn't matter that now, she knew this would end.

It didn't matter because it was too much in all the ways she'd grown to adore. It was too wicked, too impossible, too good.

Crete's tongue found hers and once again, he led her on that ancient dance that he had taught her.

And she knew each and every one of the steps by now. The angle of his jaw, the low, distant growling sound he made that had always made her shudder. It did again.

Deeper. Wilder.

It seemed preordained that he should have found her tonight, in this barren garden while seasons of flowers slumbered beneath their feet. It seemed right, somehow, that he would appear like one of her dreams and kiss her like this, making the choice before her—the choice she had already made, though her memories had plagued her—so stark. So desperate.

So unfair.

It was that last thought that had her pulling her mouth from his, so that their breath sawed out at once and made their own clouds.

But for once, she felt as if her own mind was remarkably clear where he was concerned. Though to make sure, she stepped back and put some space between their bodies. Better not to put her yearning for him to the test.

"This is wrong." Timoney was surprised that she could use her mouth to speak when what she wanted to do was curl into a ball and cry. Or pound actual stones to sand. Maybe both at once. "I'm engaged to marry Julian."

Crete's hard mouth curved. She would not call it a smile. "I hardly think that counts."

"How liberal you are," she replied, doing absolutely nothing to hide the bite in her voice. It felt like a weapon. Maybe the only one she could muster. "I hope you take this same position when, should you ever condescend to marry, you find your betrothed in another's arms only hours before the ceremony. Somehow I do not think you will."

"It does not count, little one, because you did not choose to marry him." That impossible dark blue gaze of his seemed to pin her back down to the stone bench behind her. "Did you?"

"Of course I had a choice." She should have left it at that. But instead, her mouth kept moving, and not in the right direction. "It might not have been a choice I liked, but I chose it. I chose Julian."

Maybe if she said it enough it would feel more like a gift and less like a noose.

"Did you indeed? Out of all the men in the world, you looked around and selected him?" Again, that curve in his mouth. That too-sharp amusement in his gaze. She wanted to claw at his face—but her hands couldn't be trusted to stick with violence. Crete continued as if she'd answered him. "Or was he rather chosen for you? Presented to you as the only option, to better serve your uncle's interests?"

"I'm astounded that you know Julian exists in the first place," she managed to say. "Or that my uncle does, for that matter. And I'm awash in pure astonishment that you have ever bothered to consider the business interests of men you so clearly disdain."

"I know other people exist, Timoney." His arrogant expression intensified. "I don't care that they exist. There's a difference."

"Only if you're a raging narcissist."

He shrugged, looking wholly unbothered by that. "Narcissists claim power that is not theirs and attempt to profit off of it by any means necessary. My power is earned. And it doesn't take more than a cursory examination of the financial pages to know that your uncle has grand ambitions."

In all the intense and heartbreaking dreams and daydreams she'd had since leaving London, Timoney had not thought to imagine what it might be like to finally see Crete again...only to discuss her uncle. Or Julian, for that matter.

She had imagined, fervently, that if he came for her, it would be to declare his undying love at last. To beg for her to come back to him. To tell her that he'd missed her terribly, that he couldn't live without her, that he would do anything if she would only come back to him...

But none of those words seemed to be forthcoming. And the longer she stared up at him, waiting for him to even hint a little in that direction—she had that little pride, apparently—the more arrogant he looked.

And the more a new sort of stone hardened into shape inside her.

"What does it matter?" She shook her head, trying to keep it clear. It didn't matter how he kissed. What mattered was how he'd disposed of her when he was done. She needed to remember it. "The choice was made."

"Unmake it," Crete urged her.

Her heart, her poor heart, broke. Then melted. Then broke anew as he reached over and cupped her face in his hands.

As if this was a romance. As if this was the part where that pretty music rose to a crescendo while the credits rolled and happiness was assured all around.

When she knew better.

"The guests are already here," she told him, furious that it was so hard to keep her voice even. To fight back the emotion that threatened to spill out from her eyes. "The contracts have already been signed."

"And yet we do not live in the Dark Ages, where such things might be considered irrevocable. Do not marry him, Timoney." His thumbs moved against her cheekbones, spreading warmth and heat spiraling through her. Once upon a time, she had confused that for affection. Once, she'd imagined that no matter what he said, moments like this told a different tale. Back then, when he'd told

her he could not love, she'd been so sure that
she knew better. Because she had known so
much love from her parents, and how could
that all have been lost forever? She had been
certain she could *show* him. "Come back to
London with me. Surely you want that more
than this."

And the truth was that Timoney wanted
nothing else.

In the distance, she could hear music from
the house, the piano's sweet melody spilling
out into the dark. Silent night. Holy night.
Yet all was not calm. She had felt nothing
for so long that it was like being much too
cold only to leap into hot water. Everything
tingled, so sharp it was very nearly painful.

In some ways, it was worse than pain.
Pain would have taken over and blocked out
everything else.

She was entirely too aware of the things
she felt.

Each and every one of the things she felt.

"You don't want me," Timoney said quietly, though she didn't want to. Oh, how she
didn't want to. But she couldn't hide behind convenient fictions any longer. If she
couldn't tell the truth now, when could she?

And if she couldn't tell the truth…who was she? "When you had me in every possible way, you threw me out."

"Timoney—"

"Have you changed your mind, Crete?" she asked him then, cutting off whatever excuse he might have offered. If, indeed, he would have bothered to make any excuses. "Have you come here to tell me that you love me, after all?"

And her curse was that even though she knew he had not—that he could not—she wished he had. That he was about to drop to his knees, make speeches, pull out a ring. Make any or all of the grand gestures she would have sworn she neither wanted nor needed…but, it turned out, she would very much have liked to have experienced. With him, the only man she had ever loved.

The only man you ever will love, a voice within her intoned.

As if her heart wasn't already broken enough.

His face didn't change. And he was such a magnificent specimen of a man. She had never seen his like, his beauty so ferocious it hurt to look upon. Yet once she had, it was impossible to look away. She felt as if he'd burned himself into her, a terrible brand, and yet the fact that she could smell her own charred flesh didn't keep her from tracing her fingers over the marks he'd left.

Again and again and again.

Something softened in his gaze, but his mouth stayed in its usual hard line.

"Come back," he said again, more command than entreaty. "I don't have to tell you how good we were together. You already know. I do not pretend to understand why you would walk willingly into a marriage that can give you nothing you need. Or want. Come back and we need never speak of this chapter again."

The longing was so intense then that surely she should have doubled over. Crumpled to the frozen ground. Cried, at the very least.

Timoney would never know how she remained upright. Her gaze clear. "I will take that as a no. Nothing has changed. Because you can't change, can you?"

She thought she might hate him, then, and that felt like an upgrade from the mess inside her. Because it was easier to be numb.

It was far easier to lock up all the things she felt far away, where none of it could torture her. Where she could observe what happened to her from a distance. Where she could feel nothing.

Now she felt everything.

Now she *felt*, and that might have been the most unforgivable thing he'd done yet.

"We don't need to change a thing," Crete said, as if he was warming to the subject. It made her wonder what he'd come here to say, if not this—but she pushed it aside. It didn't matter. None of this mattered. "It can be as it was."

"It can't be as it was." She shook her head at him. "Because I'm in love with you, Crete, and your reaction to my daring to say that out loud was to end everything. On the spot. Why would I sign up for that again?"

His expression hardened, and she knew that look. It was one she'd seen him wear often enough while tending to his many business concerns.

"Surely it is better to be with someone you love than this animated corpse who you will never love at all," he said, mildly enough, though she could see that considering gleam in his gaze.

Timoney wanted to scream at him not to imagine he could handle her the way he handled his legion of underlings.

But screaming would prove to him that she needed handling and kid gloves and all the other things that set her teeth on edge. Or would, if he had ever offered them. He hadn't before.

"On the contrary," she said, with a great, icy calm that she hadn't known she had inside her. "Far better to be in a relationship where I know exactly what I'm getting and what I can expect. Far better that than dying of loneliness with a man who could love me, but refuses. If I'm not to be loved, Crete, I'd rather not pretend. I'd rather immerse myself fully in the lovelessness."

What she didn't say was, *I would rather not break my heart all over again.*

He actually laughed. Timoney felt nothing short of murderous.

"I have never heard anything so absurd," he said. "You cannot mean it. Might as well march yourself off to a stint in a prison, no?"

Timoney did not choose to tell him that her

upcoming wedding rather felt like a prison, actually, and that she welcomed it. Better unmistakable iron bars than a touch like fire and that look in his gaze when he was inside her. Better not to avoid confusion.

"Surely you've had other mistresses who moved on to other men," she said, scowling at him. "I don't understand why this is such a surprise to you."

"It is true." Crete shrugged again and looked almost…philosophical. "But they did not love me. Many times they said they did, but it was not so. Not like you. You, Timoney, I believed."

"Your arrogance is breathtaking."

That wasn't hyperbole. She felt as if she'd fallen from a great height and had landed hard on her back, knocking all the air out of her body.

Timoney stepped back even farther, because she didn't want to. She wanted to move closer to him. She wanted to fling herself into his arms and promise him anything at all if he would simply take her back.

Did it matter if he loved her? Surely she could love him enough for the both of them…

But this was the trouble with Crete. He

felt like a dream come true, but she knew better. She'd lived it once already. This time, she knew there was no happy ending here. There was only misery—and that dispassionate look on his face gone cruel when he dismissed her.

She couldn't sign up for that again. She wouldn't. "If you've come all this way simply to tell me that you don't like the idea of my marrying Julian, it's a wasted trip. You could have saved yourself the trouble."

"What would make it something other than a waste, then?" he asked, in the silky manner that set off little fires all over her body—and also reminded her that whatever else he was, he was almost supernaturally gifted at making people do as he pleased. It was one of the reasons he had made himself too many fortunes to count.

She had never been any match for him.

But then, Timoney wasn't the same woman he'd met outside that club, was she? She was the woman who'd survived him the only way she knew how.

"You have nothing to offer me," she told him quietly. "It's Christmas Eve, Crete. This is a season of miracles, but you have none on offer. You decided long ago that you are incapable of such things, of any and all human emotion. And once your mind is made up, there's no changing it. I wouldn't dream of trying."

"But you cannot wish for this fate, Timoney," he said, his voice still a rough thread of silk against the night. "Do you think I have forgotten how you came apart in my hands? How you sobbed out my name? How you told me you might die if I did not return to you quickly enough each evening?"

She swayed on her feet, still breathless. And she didn't like him reminding her of those days, those weeks, that life. How desperate she'd been for him, always. How needy.

But he wasn't finished. "And yet you truly plan to shackle yourself to a man who will use your body to pleasure himself? You wish to endure a lifetime of his touch?"

"For all you know Julian is a marvelous lover," she threw at him.

And then, at last, she saw Crete change.

It was instant and overwhelming. As if they'd moved from a bright, sunny summer's day to a howling winter storm in the blink of an eye. He seemed to grow larger, wider.

Darker.

It took her long moments, her heart stuttering in her chest, to recognize that though it felt like he'd gone volcanic—though she could *see* the explosion all around them—he actually hadn't moved at all.

"And have you had many lovers since we parted?" he asked. Softly. So softly.

But the threat there was unmistakable.

Not that he would hurt her with his hands. That would be easier to handle, because if he was that kind of brute, she wouldn't feel so torn by this. By him. Rather that he would make his displeasure known in other ways—and heaven help her, but she didn't think she could survive that again. She wasn't entirely sure she'd survived it the first time.

Her heart was pounding so hard that she hurt. It *hurt*. And she had never been a liar. But she didn't think that any good would come of telling truths here. Not when he looked molten and dangerous, and too likely to express himself with his mouth on her body—

And no matter that her body responded enthusiastically to that notion, she couldn't let that happen. Not because she was so virtuous, but because the only way to live through this was to go cold turkey from Crete and his dangerous, intoxicating touch. That he'd kissed her tonight was bad enough. Anything more and she would be lost.

Julian wasn't anyone's idea of a savior, but there would be safety in marrying him all the same.

"A lady doesn't kiss and tell," she said, lifting her chin.

But Crete only laughed, as he closed the distance between them. "I don't believe you."

"Luckily, I don't require your belief. That's the thing about facts, Crete. They remain facts whether or not you believe in them."

There was a curve to his hard mouth. A gleam far harder in his dark gaze. "I believe in this."

Then he was kissing her again, and this time, it was as if he'd taken all that heat, all that fire, and thrown gas on it.

It was a mad spiral of sensation and need. Timoney could feel him everywhere, swirling around inside her, pooling low in her belly, and making her melt between her legs.

He bent her backward and she arched into

him, jubilant and joyful, her blood pumping out a rhythm that sounded like *At last, at last, at last.*

And it was only when a shock of cold hit the heated flesh of her breasts that she remembered herself.

Or tried.

She pushed him away again, unable to tell if she was gasping for breath or sobbing.

More likely, it was something in between. She glanced down at the bodice of the dress she wore, and readjusted it. Then pulled her cloak tight over breasts that ached, because, she knew, all they wanted was more.

All she ever wanted from Crete was more.

And she knew that as long as it was physical, he would give her all the *more* she could possibly want. More than she could handle. Almost more than she could take.

Timoney had lived like that for months. And when he'd taken all that *more* away, with such brutal finality, she'd thought it might kill her. Maybe it had killed her, in a way, because she wasn't who she'd been then. Not anymore. She couldn't pretend that she was.

Somehow, she knew that it was only possible to fall in love so heedlessly once.

Because ever after, it would be impossible to forget what it was like to crash back down to earth.

Or what it was like to live like that, in so many pieces.

She had gathered herself together and loved again after her parents died. But how could she possibly be so reckless again? She couldn't. She wouldn't.

"I can't tell you how many times I dreamed that you would come," she told him softly. "But it makes no difference, in the end. At least I know that now."

She told herself that was a kind of gift. A bit of grace in an otherwise bone-chilling December. Something she would find a way to live with, going forward.

The way he looked at her then was in no way graceful. "I think you will find it a stark difference, indeed, to wake the morning after next to find a man half in the grave heaving away on top of you."

Timoney did not particularly wish to imagine that. Some demon moved in her, however, and she found herself smiling serenely at him as if the image did not bother her at all.

"Crete." She tried to sound something like pitying, because it felt good. To pity someone other than herself. "You're too late."

His hard mouth moved. That was all. Maybe she needed to examine why it was she wanted it to mean more than it did. "That sounds a great deal like a challenge."

"It's really not." She thrust her hands deep into the pockets of her cloak, not sure that she would ever truly be warm again. Not now that he'd reminded her what true heat was like. True fire. "I do appreciate you coming here and reminding me exactly why I'm making the decision that I am."

Crete studied her. The moon came out from behind the clouds again and shone down all around them, making everything feel magical and miraculous—and a great many other things that were not true. She blamed Christmas. And him.

"You're getting married in the morning," he said, after a moment. "That means I have the whole of the night to change your mind."

And like that, she lost the ability to

breathe again. "It…absolutely does not mean that."

His eyes glinted with a hint of heat. "I don't mind telling you, little one. I like my chances."

"What do you think will happen? Do you think you're going to so muddle my head with sex that I'll forget what you did to me? That you had me bodily removed from your flat?" And she still couldn't breathe, but it turned out, she didn't care about that as much as she could have. As much as she should have. "Because let me assure you, Crete. I won't forget that. Ever."

"Forget or do not forget," he said with a shrug. A *shrug*. "All I ask is that you allow me to remind you of everything else."

Timoney couldn't understand why he wanted to do this. It didn't make sense, not after the night he'd so cruelly tossed her aside. When he'd been brutally clear that there was no future here, no matter what.

She stared at him in the mist and moonlight, that beautiful face of his set and unreadable, the way it always was.

And she reminded herself that she had survived him. She had survived that night, though she'd thought it might kill her. Dead inside though she may have felt, she had not, in fact, died. She wasn't the same woman he'd crushed so easily.

And she was marrying Julian tomorrow, no matter what he did tonight.

If, as she suspected, the light of day would remind Crete how little he wanted the things he seemed to think he wanted here in the dark, that was fine.

What would it hurt to treat this as a little exercise in wish fulfillment until then? She wasn't susceptible to him now—not the way she had been, anyway. She could have lost herself completely in him only moments ago, but she hadn't. She'd found her footing. She'd held it.

And this was the first time she'd been around him for more than a few minutes without the passion between them erupting, rolling on into that same inferno no matter where they were. The cloakroom of a club. Too many vehicles to count. The bathroom at an upscale restaurant with most of fashionable London on the other side of the door.

There you go, she told herself. *It's already different. You're fully clothed.*

She told herself that the heat she felt inside her then was shame. And then felt a tiny ribbon of real shame, because it wasn't.

"You'd better come into the house," Timoney told him, after a moment. After making sure she felt steady enough with the invitation. "But you mustn't be seen."

Then she whirled around and started back up the cold stone path, not checking to see if he followed her.

For she knew that he did.

Like something out of a Greek myth.

Are you afraid that if you look back that he'll be gone? she asked herself as she walked. *Or that he won't?*

She led him to one of the doors on the far side of the manor that led to the conservatory, where no one but Timoney ever seemed to go. Her uncle and his guests had moved into one of the sitting rooms, as she'd seen through the brightly lit windows, and she couldn't think of a reason any of them would venture away from the warmth and the drink to come all the way across into the old part of the house.

It would be safer to take Crete to her bedchamber, where she could lock the door, but she hoped she wasn't quite *that* foolish.

Once inside, she sat down on her favorite settee, where she'd spent hours and hours as a child. And she wasn't prepared for the sight of Crete, then, prowling around this particular room as if he was altering her childhood with every step. He was so male. So reckless and bold in this place she thought of as soft. Sweet.

She told herself it was a rude intrusion, that was all. He didn't belong here. He belonged in that flat of his, sharp and chilly. Not in a room of books and cozy throws, soft woven rugs, and the promise of plants come spring.

Timoney ignored that melting sensation, molten hot between her legs, that suggested she was interested in other intrusions, the ruder the better.

This was for her, she reminded herself sternly. She would indulge Crete, but only to please herself. Because she hadn't imagined she would ever be alone with him again. And this was her opportunity to ask him all the things she'd always wanted to know, but had been too afraid—or perhaps too over-awed—to ask while they'd been together.

And this time, he might actually answer.

He might deny it, but she knew that he would leave. Possibly as soon as he realized that she was not the girl he'd known. That he'd made her into the woman she was now, and he might not like what that meant.

But before he understood that shift, he would answer a few questions.

Like the one she'd asked the version of him she carried around in her head every night since she'd last seen him.

"So. Crete." She cleared her throat. "Why are you like this?"

CHAPTER FOUR

IT TOOK CRETE a moment or two to process that question.

He stopped moving around the graceful room she'd led him into. It gave the sense of genteel clutter and faded glory, from the arched glass windows that curved up overhead to the battered old carpets tossed this way and that across the floor. Betraying the sort of carelessness that went along with generational wealth, he thought.

It was only when your great-grandfather had carted that rug back from the mystical lands where he'd found it, and your grandmother had used it in her dressing room, that you might carry on and fling it on the floor beneath a great mess of planters.

Still, he couldn't work up his usual disdain for these people who thought the world

had been built for their pleasure. Because
the books on the overstuffed shelves that
lined the back wall were not the fancy hard-
backs with gold embossing on the spines
that he always thought looked fake. They
seemed to be popular in the supposed librar-
ies a certain sort of man always seemed to
have scattered about the old stately home,
though Crete had never been able to imagine a person actually using such a place for
anything but attempting to intimidate.

But this room was different. It felt like
Timoney.

"Is this your room?" he asked, because it
had her air, somehow. Did he actually smell
wildflower honey, or was he imagining it?
All the books on the shelves were well read.
He could see the swollen, cracked spines of
thick, fat paperbacks. He picked up a battered hardcover at random and found the
pages worn from turning.

This was like a view inside of her, and he
had avoided that. Had gone out of his way
to avoid that, in point of fact. This was an
intimacy. And Crete had always preferred
that his intimacies remain only and ever
physical.

"My mother used to grow her favorite plants here," Timoney told him, a distant sort of look in her eyes, as if she was looking off into a beloved past. That, too, seemed like an intimate moment. Or maybe it was that he, personally, had no experience with any past that wasn't harsh. So much so that, any time she had attempted to talk about the parents she so clearly loved, he had prevented her. Usually by stoking the fires between them as he would have dearly liked to do now. But he did not. Because if she wished to discuss her mother, he would grit his teeth and allow her to make her mother real for him. No matter how uncomfortable it made him. "She was no gardener, but she liked to putter about with the odd herb and an occasional hardy geranium. She would play with potting soil and seeds in the sunlight and I would read."

The look on her face was so open then. So naked. Something seized in his chest at the sight, and he told himself it was concern for her, that was all. That she should show such softness to another. That she would allow herself such recklessness and let it infect the whole of her face.

That she should let anyone see her feelings like this. Even him. *Especially* him.

She sniffed as she regarded him, her expression suddenly much less soft. "You haven't answered the question."

He looked at the shelves of books again, a vast selection of all genres with colorful covers and yellowing pages, trying to imagine Timoney here. As a small child, as young girl, as a sulky teenager. And with a mother who wanted to spend time with her—or, at least, did not actively avoid it.

The notion was like folklore. He dismissed it.

"Why am I like what?" he asked. Coolly.

He turned to face her again, and they were indoors now. This room was far brighter than the moonlight out in the garden. The lamps she'd turned on as she entered, finding them so easily in the dark that he should have known precisely how comfortable she was here, cast a buttery light all around. He had told himself, in that moment before she'd switched on the first light, that the spell would be broken. That the creature he'd seen out there in the dark was not the enchantress she'd seemed in that swirling red cloak, as much mist as moon.

But of course, in the light, it was worse.

She made his mouth go dry.

Timoney still wore her cloak, swirled around her like some kind of blanket. She pulled her feet up beneath her and she should have looked like a child, sitting there on that little couch of hers while she gazed up at him with her blue eyes so solemn.

Almost accusatory.

But she did not look like a little girl at all. Even inside, she looked as if the moon was in her hair. She was elfin, unworldly. Her blond hair was silvery as it fell about her shoulders, cascading down from two pearlescent combs. Her chin was pointed just enough to make her face the shape of a heart. And there was that perfect bow of a mouth of hers, generous and sensual, that he had tasted a thousand times. Yet he still wanted more.

He had accepted that truth, uncomfortable as it was, out there in the dark.

Or he had stopped fighting it. Surely that was the same thing.

"Everybody knows your story," Timoney

said after a moment. In a careful sort of way, as if she was choosing her words with precision. As if he required such handling.

He bristled at that notion. "Do they indeed? Am I so easily digested, then?"

"What you tell of your story, anyway," she amended, a considering sort of look on her face. "Your mother met your father when she was very young and he was on a business trip to Athens."

Crete would never understand why the everyday squalid details of his parents' lives were a subject of such fascination to other people. When what mattered, to his mind, was never the hand he'd been dealt but what games he'd learned to play—and win—with those cards.

"My father had the affair," he said now. Perhaps too brusquely. "He was married. My mother was foolish perhaps, but all she did was follow her heart. She was eighteen. He was thirty-four. I tell you this only because their age gap is always mentioned, as if it alone is what caused all the trouble."

Timoney looked almost dreamy. "I think many people forget that eighteen feels quite worldly and grown up. To the person experiencing it."

Crete found himself leaning back against the nearest bookshelf and thrusting his hands deep in the pockets of his trousers, because it was that hard to keep them to himself. He tried to remember other times that he and Timoney had sat about talking, but none came to mind.

Because when they were in the same room together, it had always been about that passion. About that need. He could feel it inside him, bright and greedy.

Outside, he'd intended to indulge in that passion. That greed. To use it to prove what he already knew. That she was his—whatever that meant. And that whatever happened, she certainly wasn't going to marry a lascivious old tosser like Julian Browning-Case. He had felt certain that the best way to make his point was by reminding her exactly how good it was between them. As acrobatically as possible.

But he hadn't gotten where he was by being unable to read a room. It was obvious to him that Timoney believed he wasn't capable of talking. That this was a challenge.

And Crete had never backed down from a challenge.

He wasn't about to start now.

"I do not disagree with you," he said after a moment. "After all, I was cast out into the world at eighteen myself. No one seemed concerned about whether or not I felt ready. I was expected to be a man, therefore I was." He lifted a shoulder, then dropped it. "But my mother had been very sheltered up until that point. She was not prepared."

He said that with authority, though all he knew about his mother had come to him secondhand. Some of what he knew had come from the very articles he disliked, because his mother's family had allowed reporters access they had always refused him.

Until he became so infamous the world over that they'd changed their tune. Which had allowed him to refuse them all in turn. The circle of life was a circle of spite, he had always believed. And he had never been afraid to prove it.

But somehow he did not want to express it in quite that way to this magical creature, who, unlike everyone else, never looked at him as if he was an alien. Crete normally did not care how others regarded him. He often encouraged them to imagine he was not quite human.

It was different to imagine Timoney doing the same. The notion made him...*feel*.

And it was an unpleasant feeling. He preferred her to regard him as if he might, in fact, be the sun.

He had come to depend on it.

"You lost her when you were two years old," Timoney said, and though it was a statement, he could see the question in her blue gaze.

"Do you wish to tell me my own story?" he asked her. "Or are you waiting for me to tell you things it seems you already know?"

He hated that her gaze turned...sympathetic. "Do I know the real story, Crete? Does anyone?"

Crete found himself rubbing at his chest, and dropped his hand like it was lit on fire. He didn't understand why he was indulging her like this. A challenge, yes. But as much as he didn't walk away from challenges, he was also justly famous for changing rules he didn't like to suit himself. What he knew was that he didn't want her to marry tomorrow.

But why was he subjecting himself to… this?

It wasn't that he didn't spend his time chatting with women. Crete didn't spend any time chatting. With anyone. At all. He knew that other men had friends. Warmer associations with others. The odd golf buddy. But he had never seen the allure in such connections.

And he didn't particularly care for the fact that this woman had seemed to zero right in on the *why* of it.

Crete had always taken such pride in the idea that nobody knew him at all.

"I don't remember her," he told Timoney now. Because the only thing worse, to his mind, than telling her his personal details was the idea that she might think he was afraid to do it. When he was afraid of nothing. Not even the sad truth of the end of his mother's life. Abandoned by her lover, then her family. Unable to care for her child when she was little more than a child herself. Was it any wonder she had chosen despair and drink? A slower suicide than some, but a suicide all the same. "That seems monstrous, perhaps, but as you say, she died when I was two. Her parents had disowned her when she fell pregnant."

Timoney made a soft noise. It sounded like distress. Possibly...for him?

Crete did not attempt to parse that, or why it echoed in him like a kind of pain. He also did not permit his hand to rise again to his chest. "The legend goes like this. After burying his only daughter, my grandfather took her son to the doorstep of the man he blamed for his daughter's dark spiral, and left him there."

"You mean you," Timoney said softly. "He left you there."

"I am told this is a sad tale, but for me, I have always liked it." Crete shrugged. "It is like the ancient Spartans, is it not? He laid me out to see if the wolves would take me. Perhaps he expected me to die. But instead, I thrived."

As he always did. As he always would.

"Did he really leave you on a doorstep in Oslo?"

"He did." Crete was uncomfortable. Stiff. When he had learned over time that others usually displayed signs of discomfort when he told stories about himself. It was why he'd stopped doing it a long time ago. But she had asked, had she not? Even if she looked...well. Not as uncomfortable as he felt. "Luckily it was summer. My father's wife found me. And who can say how long I was there? I've heard it told many ways. An hour, perhaps, in one reckoning. Overnight, according to another. But however long it was, my father's wife opened the door eventually. And saw before her a toddler with jet black hair and her husband's eyes. She knew at once who I must be. And it would have been so easy to turn away, but she did not. She took me in."

"Who would turn away from an abandoned toddler on their doorstep?" Timoney asked, shaking her head as if he'd said something funny. "I have heard you give this version of events before, you know, and I cannot understand it. As if your father's wife was some kind of saint for...not leaving you to die."

"Was she not? To take in her husband's bastard? Who else would do such a thing?"

"I think it's very human to wish to help

a child." Timoney studied him, frowning slightly, and he chose not to wonder what she saw. "And did she actually take you in?"

"That is where I lived for the next sixteen years."

"That is where you lived, yes. And from where you were summarily ejected on your eighteenth birthday, never to return. Isn't that right?"

He found that his jaw was so tight it actually hurt. "Yes."

Timoney nodded as if he'd confirmed her worst fears. "Did your father's wife take you in out of the goodness of her heart? Because she is some sainted creature? Or did she do it to rub your father's nose in what he did?" When he didn't respond, she blew out a breath. "A less saintly motivation, I think. And not particularly kind to the child caught in the crossfire."

Crete did not often permit himself to descend into memories of his childhood. Because he already knew that nothing good waited there. And perhaps because of that, he had always been focused on the only thing that was ever his. His future.

"What interests me, Timoney," he said

now. And with intent. "Is that you asked me to tell you my story, did you not? And yet you are now arguing with me about it."

"I've read great many articles about you." Another woman might have flushed at that admission. But not Timoney. She kept her gaze trained on his in a manner he would have called challenging if it was anyone else. Anyone at all but this woman, who had only ever melted in his arms. He could not quite see her in any other way. He did not wish to. "And they all hit the same notes. Callous grandparents. Lost mother. The long-suffering wife who overlooked her husband's infidelity to raise you almost as her own."

"They all tell that story because it's true." She didn't shift her gaze away at his fierce tone. Something in him thudded. Hard. "Are you suggesting that I have lied about my own history?"

And it said something—though nothing he wished to acknowledge—that he questioned himself for a moment. That she sat there looking like moonlight and the Mediterranean, and he wondered, if only for a moment, if she knew more about his childhood than he did.

"I don't think you're a liar," she said. "But that doesn't mean I think you're telling the truth, either."

All of this was settling on him in a way Crete could only call uncomfortable. It was because she didn't look dazed or dizzy at the sight of him, the way she always had before. It was because she wasn't flushed and prettily begging for his touch. Nor did she look crushed, the way she had that last night.

Instead, Timoney was looking at him coolly, as if examining a specimen.

He couldn't say he cared for that at all.

And not only because he could not recall anyone looking at him like that in a very long while. Certainly not since he had become the Crete Asgar the world liked to whisper about in tones of awe behind the very hands they held out to him.

"Am I not?" he asked, though he didn't want to know. But he didn't want her to see how very little he wanted to know.

"You are closed off in every way," she replied, her gaze intent and her voice quiet. And had she sat up straighter, like some oracle delivering bad news? "Locked up tight. If you have any emotions at all, you only let them out by having sex. Everything else is off-limits. You make money and you make love, though I doubt very much you would call it that. And that's it. You act as if there's nothing else to you. And that cannot be, can it? No one is so stark or uncomplicated. Especially those that pretend otherwise."

He found he was more tense than he should have been. When normally he laughed off attempts to attack him or psychoanalyze him in turn, because his foes might as well throw stones at the moon. Yet she was not a foe. And it felt too much like her stones were landing. "You seem to believe that simple truths about me are accusations, Timoney. When perhaps what they are is a bit of wishful thinking on the part of a scorned woman, no?"

That was not exactly the smart way to play this, but the words seemed to come out of him of their own accord. As if he had somehow lost the control that had always defined him.

But instead of reacting badly to being called a scorned woman, Timoney only smiled.

As if she, elfin and unearthly, was the one

in control here. An insupportable notion, but Crete did nothing to challenge it. Almost as if he…didn't want to challenge it.

"No one is that compartmentalized," she said after a moment.

As if she, too, expected him to do something. To challenge her, maybe. Or to do what he had always done when she'd lived with him—cross the room and get his hands on her, forestalling any possibility of a discussion. Almost as if he'd done it deliberately.

Had he?

But there was no time to answer that, thankfully, because she was considering him much too closely from her perch on the small sofa. "And if you think that you are, in fact, precisely that uncomplicated, then there's no reason at all for you to be here. Is there? Because interfering in an ex-lover's wedding is, I think you'll find, the very definition of *messy*."

Crete straightened from the bookshelf, but slowly. He did not take his eyes off Timoney, who was still sitting there looking innocent and unruffled as if she hadn't set a trap and walked him right into it.

He really should have been impressed. Instead of…tense.

"I am as possessive of my money as I am about my women," he growled at her. "If that is what you mean."

"We both know *that* is not true." She tilted her head to one side, her eyes bright. Very, very bright. "One thing I think the whole world knows about you and your many women is that you are the very opposite of possessive. Or so a great many of them have complained. In the tabloids. Repeatedly."

"You did not."

"I did not," she agreed.

And he did not care for the solemn way she looked at him then.

Crete wanted to go to her. He wanted to show her exactly how possessive he was of *this* woman, anyway. But there was something in the cool, steady way she was regarding him that told him she expected him to do just that.

And he intensely disliked the idea that he was in any way predictable. Especially to her.

He moved away from the well-loved books toward the selection of colorful pots arranged over a thickly tiled table set before one of the great windows. The pots were all empty and the window was cold enough that he could feel it from several feet away, as if the winter was pressed against the glass. And he could not have said why it was that the sight of so many pots, empty of their supposed herbs and occasional plucky blooms, made him ache.

Crete would have claimed, before tonight, that he was incapable of *aching*.

"Why don't you tell me my story, then," he said, his voice as dark as the thick Christmas Eve outside. Because he could see her reflection in the glass before him, and the ache in him only grew. "You know it better than I do, apparently. But I must warn you, Timoney. When you're finished, I might just return the favor."

"I think you're lonely," she said, and for all her voice was soft, the words still stung. "I think your father's wife made certain you were never comfortable in her home. She made sure you were always made to feel different. Always her charity case. Always expected to be grateful for the crumbs of her affection."

"You are mistaken." His gaze was on the collection of empty pots before him. A blue one in particular, with leftover dirt clinging to the clay. And he reminded himself that he was relaying facts, that was all. Only the facts. "There were no such crumbs. There was no affection."

"She strikes me as a deeply bitter woman who kept you so she might better punish her straying husband. And it's striking to me that you never speak of him. The man who abandoned your mother, did not claim you until he had no other option, and was happy enough to see the back of you when his wife determined that she had done enough of her duty."

"He is a weak man, yes." He ran a finger over the raised edge of the pot's wide mouth. Once. Again. He did not think of his tall, blond, disinterested father. Because what point was there in it? "But surely that goes without saying. Look at what he did."

"But how does it *feel*, Crete?" Timoney asked in the same devastatingly quiet way. "You're a grown man now. You've gone to such trouble to make your way in the world. And I know it's a story you tell, but how does it feel? How did it feel when you were just a kid and treated differently than your half siblings?"

He turned toward her then, incredulous. "What does it matter how it felt? Feelings don't change anything."

They had never changed anything. Not his cold childhood, always given less than his brother and sister. Not nothing, but less. So that no one could ever forget that he was not the same as them.

Their father had never intervened. He had never spoken to Crete at all, if he could help it. And whatever his wife did or said, he supported it.

Crete had felt a great deal about all of that, at the time. And those feelings had done nothing but make his misery the worse.

It was when he'd ignored what he felt and concentrated on what he could *do* that everything had changed. Not his situation. Not his tormentors. But his reactions to them.

Change yourself and you change the world, he liked to tell himself.

He was living proof.

"Feeling is who we are," Timoney was saying, her voice...intense.

"I prefer facts."

"All facts tell us is what happened," she retorted. "Not what it was like."

"I do not wish to remember what it was like." And the words seemed to come from somewhere inside him he would have sworn wasn't there. Because he'd torn it out a lifetime ago and filled it with other, better things, like the infinite pleasures of the flesh. Still, he kept his distance from Timoney, with her elfin face and too much wisdom in her eyes like the sea. "Why would I want to remember such things? I already lived through it once."

She only waited, and he didn't understand what was happening. The woman he'd taken as his mistress had given him her innocence, and everything after that had been an exercise in yielding. The softness and sweetness of it, all her smiles and surrenders.

Had she always been this way underneath? How had he failed to notice it before now?

Crete wanted to go. Now. If he was king of anything, it was a well-timed retreat before coming back harder. Stronger.

He had the strangest sensation that he was out of his depth here, with her—

But he refused to indulge such nonsense.

He refused to indulge any of this nonsense.

"It is as you say," he told her, his voice rougher than before. "My father's wife used me to bludgeon him. An effective weapon, I think, as there is no evidence he ever strayed again. Meanwhile, my mother's grim legend of a father died when I was ten. And any notion I might have nurtured, that the other members of my mother's family might take a softer approach to my existence, was quickly extinguished. For they blamed me as much for his death as for hers."

She breathed something. He thought it was his name.

"Do you wish me to tell you that it was a bitter childhood? Lonely years spiced up only by disdain and contempt?" He laughed, and jerked his chin to take in this room they stood in, still warm from the very different childhood she'd had. "Unlike you, I have nothing to compare it to. And those years made me who I am today, Timoney. How can I resent them?"

"But you do," she said quietly, frowning at him. "Deeply, I think."

"You're mistaken."

He didn't mean to move. He didn't know it when he did. All Crete knew was that one moment he'd been across the room and the next he stood above her, staring down at where she sat—looking as wildly innocent as the night he'd first touched her.

Maybe he should have known then that she would be a terrible problem.

"This is why I do not tell the real story of how it was," he gritted down at her. At that lovely face of hers that had haunted him across two full months. And half a year before that. "This is what happens. Softhearted, emotional people like yourself imagine that they must infuse it all with pathos. With incurable grief. While for me, those years were an opportunity. A crucible, if you will. I survived them, I became me, and if anything, I am grateful to my father and his wife and even my bitter old grandfather, for making certain that I never, ever succumb to the petty emotions of the human heart."

But as he watched too much emotion fill

her blue gaze, then, nothing about it felt petty at all.

"And the only reason you could possibly be here is that you don't like sharing your toys, is that what you're trying to tell me?" Her voice was little more than a whisper, her sea-colored eyes luminous. "That's not a very good reason, is it?"

He wanted to rage at her that she was no toy. That if she was a mere toy, he would have forgotten her as surely and as quickly as the rest.

"We'll get to that in due time," Crete promised her, grimly. But inside him, a different kind of storm brewed. Electric and more than a little mad. "But first, little one, let us speak of you."

CHAPTER FIVE

"I'M THE ONE asking the questions," Timoney protested, but her words seemed to trail off even as she was speaking them.

Because Crete levered himself down, bracing his hands on the back of the settee, effectively caging her there.

Unless, of course, she wanted to lean forward and—

But no. That would be bad.

Because it would be so good.

And Timoney was unprepared for this, if she was honest. It had been bad enough for him to appear out of the mist, like every dream she'd had since she'd left his flat in London in tears. It had been another to sit on this well-worn couch she loved, to gather her strength around her as securely as she had her cloak and imagine this was some kind of cross-examination.

One she might actually win.

Especially when she'd gotten him to do a thing he'd never, ever done before—talk about himself. Not his businesses, but *him*.

It was a harsh little gift, but a gift all the same.

She had always suspected he was a man who *could* feel deeply. She had always told herself that, secretly, he did. But having heard him actually discuss the cold facts of his stark upbringing, she wasn't at all surprised that he didn't want to.

Timoney felt entirely too much on his behalf.

But now his face was too close to hers. And that same old familiar seismic upheaval that was a hallmark of the Crete Asgar experience rocked through her anew. There was no solid ground. There was only the brilliant dark blue of his eyes, his perfectly sculpted face, and that scraped-raw, hollowed-out-with-longing need for him that she didn't think she would ever be rid of.

No matter what happened tomorrow.

"You were soft and spoiled when I found

you," he said, his voice as pitiless as it was rough, and yet she felt it on her skin—all over her skin—like a caress. She had to fight to repress a shudder of reaction. "A ripe little peach, mine for the taking. If it hadn't been me, little one, it could have been anyone. You and those useless friends of yours, careening about London, looking for trouble. Do you know how many girls like you find more trouble than they can handle, year after year?"

"Do *you*?" she retorted, though her heartbeat was heavy in her ears and her skin felt so oversensitive that a glance might make her come apart. "And if you do, it really begs the question—how many young women do you normally pluck up and carry off into coatrooms?"

His mouth curved and it was not a relief. It was too hard for that. Too sardonic.

"Here's what I know about entitled little heiresses like you," he said, his voice a raw thread of dark need inside her. That was the trouble with this man. He had always felt like he was a part of her. "You spin around brightly, then crash. One after the next. Whether it is into sad marriages like the one you plan to enter into tomorrow. Whether it is too much partying, too much exposure, too much glamour, until all you can see is the underside of such things, black and scarred and torn. It all ends in the same dreary way."

"If I'm so interchangeable, there seems even less of a reason that you should find yourself here tonight," she managed to say, somehow getting her chin to lift in at least some small show of defiance. No matter how shaky she felt inside. "Go find another just like me, with my compliments. I'm sure she can tell you exactly what you want to hear. Sooner or later you'll almost certainly find one who won't dare to express emotion in your sterile little apartment no matter the provocation. A match made in heaven."

"This is the point I'm trying to make, little one," he murmured, still much too close. Still too raw, inside and out. Could she feel the heat of his body, blazing into her? Or was it that she wished she could? "Girls like you are used to getting what you desire. You don't even know how to want, not really. The world is simply handed to you on one platter after another, so that you truly believe it's character building to live in Belgravia in a listed house. You may even think you're roughing it when really, all you're doing is playacting until your money comes in."

As that hewed a bit too close to her own thoughts on her tenure as an admittedly silly PR girl, she had no choice but to bristle at hearing *him* say it.

"Thank you for your dissertation on my uselessness," she threw back at him. "But I assure you, no one is more aware of the playacting component than me."

"You should thank me for throwing you out, Timoney." And his dark blue eyes glittered like the night sky. "It looks as if it's given you a little bit of character."

What was funny was that she knew that was meant to be a killing blow. If he had delivered it while they'd been together, it would have destroyed her.

But that was the thing about being wrecked as totally as he had wrecked her. It wasn't possible to be wrecked like that twice.

Or she hoped it wasn't.

So she did the unthinkable. She laughed. "It seems to me that you're indicting yourself," she said. "Maybe it's true that I was an unformed little piece of clay, traipsing about London in search of meaning or a kiln. But it's also true that you were captivated by that particular little lump of earth. Besotted, one might even say. But not in love, of course." And she did nothing to keep that faint note of mockery from her voice. Maybe not so faint. "Because that would be a bridge too far. Did you come here to see if you can erase the damage you did so I can go straight back to being putty in your hands?"

"I would not object."

His gaze dropped to her mouth, then, and try as she might, Timoney couldn't deny the electricity that hummed within her. Maybe she didn't want to deny it.

But whatever backbone she might have gathered on her way out of London, she knew she might as well rip it out and sling it out into the snow if she succumbed to his kisses again.

Twice tonight was already too much. It made her much too weak. Too susceptible.

She ducked under his arm and rolled to her feet, not caring if he knew she was legitimately running away from him. She was.

Because she knew exactly how shaky her foundation was when he was concerned.

"Insulting me isn't going to change the fact that I have more questions for you," she told him when she was standing some distance away. "If that's what you thought."

"I did not intend to insult you. And I've answered your questions. You are the one who has flung herself halfway across the room a great deal, as if you fear something. Is it me, *Timonitsa mou*? Or is it yourself?"

Timonitsa mou. My little Timoney.

"Very well." She could feel herself flushing hot, and knew that it was entirely possible that he could see it. That was unfortunate. But she didn't understand what she could do to stop it, so she simply slipped out of her cloak, and tossed it over the back of the settee, a little shower of bright red fabric to distract them both. "Let us speak of fear. To the casual observer, it would appear that you're the one who's afraid. Of the possibility I might love you. Or is it something more than that? Is it...?" She dared to look back at him then, searching his face and that faintly arrested expression he wore. "Is it more that you're afraid you might actually love me back?"

Timoney couldn't believe she'd dared ask that question.

It was as if all the air in the room was sucked away, and there was nothing but the beat of her heart. And of his, too, though perhaps she only imagined she could hear it. Feel it.

Like he was always going to be a part of her.

She saw his jaw tense. There was a flicker of movement, and she glanced down to see his hands in fists at his sides.

And Timoney couldn't tell in that moment if she wanted to push him further, to see if he would break—

Or if she wanted only to hold him and mend his jagged pieces back together as best as she could, with whatever tools she had to hand—

But there was a sound in the hall outside the conservatory, and to her horror, she realized that she could hear voices.

And worse, they were drawing closer.

"You cannot be found here," she hissed at Crete.

One of his arrogant brows rose and she thought he intended to refuse to hide himself. To stand his ground and face whoever came in the door, and everything inside her…eased, a little, at that notion.

Because if it happens, you will have to choose, won't you? asked a voice inside her. *If it is your uncle, he will know exactly what this means, and he will demand—*

But it didn't matter. Because, perhaps more astonishing than anything that had come before, Crete looked around and then stalked over to that long table where her mother had kept all of her pots. It was sturdy and tiled, and it was impossible to look beneath it, thanks to all the terra-cotta pots still stacked there.

She blinked in astonishment as Crete… disappeared behind it, lowering himself between the table and the window with tremendous, offended dignity.

On any list of things Crete Asgar might do, she would never in her life have included any possibility that he might secrete himself behind a table. For any reason at all.

It made her feel something like dizzy.

Out in the hallway, the voices moved

closer. Timoney looked around, snatched a book off the shelf, then retreated to her settee and did her best to look as if she was entrenched in her reading.

Only moments later the door was flung open and a couple came tumbling in, laughing and flushed with as much wine as ardor.

And it was from some great distance inside, some bird's-eye view, that Timoney recognized the pair of them. It was Julian, who was to marry her come the morning. And the young wife of some minor diplomat.

Julian came to a stop. He stared at Timoney, who stared back.

In mute astonishment.

The diplomat's wife took longer, and when she recognized the bride—the reason she was here in this house at all—she only glanced at Julian and quietly excused herself.

After she shut the door behind her, all was silent.

Timoney dared not glance over at her mother's potting table.

"I say, my dear," said Julian in that same voice that he always used, that Timoney liked to tell herself was *courtly*. When she thought the real word to describe it was *condescending*. "I rather thought you'd retired for the evening."

"I like to read each evening before I sleep." She glanced down at the book in her lap and saw that she'd picked out one of her favorite books, a thick volume of children's adventure stories that actually featured girls, not boys.

She wanted to club him with it.

Which was in itself a surprise, as it was the most she'd felt in Julian's presence since they'd met.

Julian studied her for a moment, then smiled in a manner that looked diffident and apologetic. That was, unless she looked at his cold gaze, which was neither.

"I am a man of many needs, my dear," he said then, in the same tone. "A conversation I expected to have after our wedding, not before. But you are a practical girl, are you not? You must be, I think, to marry so quickly after such a scandalous union as the one you had with Asgar. As you know, I have already indicated that I will care for any...unfortunate consequences of that union." He nodded at her belly, as if she might have missed his meaning. "I ask very little in return."

"That *very little* being a blind eye, presumably," she said. "To diplomat's wives and whoever else catches your fancy. Is that it?"

He inclined his head. "I'm of an old school. I will require all the usual marital rights, but in a situation such as ours, where there are no complications involving tender feelings, it can truly harm no one if I slake some of my darker hungers in other places. You may learn to thank me for this, in time." That smile of his deepened, though his gaze seemed harder. "You seem at a loss for words, Timoney."

"It's all so indelicate," she said quietly, like the girl she'd been pretending to be for months. Encased in ice and irritated when anything disturbed her bleakness. But now everything was different. Now she had melted. Still, she tried. "Surely such things are not spoken of. Not like this."

"Now, now," Julian said, with a chuckle that was not in the least bit friendly. "Fewer lessons in decorum from a girl who until recently was nothing but a whore for a mongrel, please."

Her blood pounded so hard in her ears that Timoney was shocked she didn't topple over. It took every bit of willpower she had to keep from whipping her head around to see if Crete was reacting to that *mongrel* comment from his place behind the table.

She wanted to scream.

She wanted to fly at Julian and slap him straight across his red, jowly face.

It was as if she'd emerged from some kind of frigid swamp. She'd thought of it as being frozen solid, but what she felt now was far worse than a simple melting. It threatened to suck her in, this realization of what she'd done. What she'd agreed to when she'd felt nothing.

Had Julian said such things before? Had he expressed his opinion about not only Crete but also Timoney's behavior like this?

She couldn't remember it, because she hadn't cared either way. And yet she knew, suddenly and without doubt, that he had.

And more, that she'd simply sat there like a block of icy wood, too lost in her own misery to care what was said to her or around her.

God help her, but this brutal awakening was not a kindness.

"I see the cat has got your tongue," Julian said with another chuckle. "This pleases me, Timoney. I don't mind telling you, I'm not marrying you for your conversation."

His gaze raked over her then, making her feel stripped naked. And not in a pleasant way. Not the way she felt when Crete looked at her, too much heat in his gaze.

It felt rather more like a threat.

She actually bit her own tongue to keep from speaking any of the words that clambered there, desperate to fall out of her mouth.

Or more likely catapult out and insult this man, who she was only just realizing she didn't know at all.

Not because he hadn't showed himself to her. But because she hadn't been paying attention.

"Enjoy your reading," he told her. "I shall see you in the morning."

Another threat.

Timoney stayed where she was until she

heard the faintest sound from behind her, only a breath after the door closed behind Julian.

She turned, almost afraid, so wildly did her heart pound.

For Crete rose from the place where he had concealed himself, a dark movement. And his gaze upon her was like thunder.

She expected him to seethe at her. Possibly even shout. She expected him to storm across the room and grab her, hauling her up against him to argue his case.

And the contrast between the man who had just walked out of this room and Crete there before her was almost too much to bear. Especially when all he did was stand there instead of moving closer, that blue gaze dark and intent on her.

Meaning she could not help but compare the man she loved with the man she would marry.

It was painful.

More than painful. It made her stomach twist viciously, so that she almost doubled over. It made a kind of sick shame wash over her. It made her feet seem to lose their grip on the floor beneath her, like she might tumble off into nothing, and she did not know if she wanted to scream or cry. Or both.

She had known the differences between the two men, of course. It wasn't as if she hadn't noticed them before. How could anyone fail to notice them?

But she had never gazed upon Julian with Crete's taste in her mouth.

"Well?" she demanded, because that was better than the silence. "Will you delight me with more trenchant observations about who I am and why I've made the choices I have?"

His mouth flattened. "I think your choices speak for themselves."

And that was worse.

Timoney's eyes eased closed and she found herself wrapping her arms around her middle, as if that could do something. As if she could hug herself out of this.

"Do you require that I say this again?" came his voice. Dark. Silken and rough at once and worse, inevitable. Irrevocable. "You cannot marry that man, Timoney. You must know this."

Timoney had never known anything more. And she sucked in a breath, prepared to tell him that, no matter how reckless—

But she stopped herself.

Because there were other things she knew.

And one of them was him.

She had long wanted to ask him about his childhood, and while he hadn't told her anything tonight she hadn't known already, that he'd told her anything at all felt like a revolution. Because while he had spent their time together splitting his focus between her and his many businesses, she had done absolutely nothing but study him. It was one more thing she'd beat herself up about once he'd dropped her.

But her studies hadn't been in vain—because he'd shown her that he did feel. As deeply as she'd known he did. She'd heard his battered heart in every gruff word he'd uttered.

Timoney still believed with everything she was, every bone in her body, that he loved her. But so what? What did Crete Asgar know of love?

Not only did she doubt that he could identify his own emotions, she doubted it would matter if he did. If she were to do as he asked, walk away from this wedding, move in with him again, even attempt to hammer out some kind of relationship that was less one-sided than the one they'd had before… What would it accomplish?

There would be more time with him, yes. And that was no small thing. She thought there was a part of her that would gladly sell her own soul for even one day more. At her lowest point, she would have made that bargain for a mere glimpse of him from across a road.

But she already knew how it would end.

And what she'd told him out in the garden had not changed.

It was a shame that she felt alive again, so that the devil she knew seemed a whole lot more like a demon she hadn't fully comprehended until now.

But Julian had already given her the schematics to the marriage he expected. All she had to do was follow the rules. There would be no emotional cost. Sex would be unpleasant, but then, wasn't that what she wanted? Because she'd already had far too much of the kind of lovemaking that made her soul feel too thin. That had not only taken her apart with pleasure, but had made her wonder how it was possible to exist in a world when she was so profoundly changed.

She had to think it was better for her to subject herself to Julian's attentions rather than go back to Crete only to lose herself, then him, all over again.

Because she also knew that Julian's attentions would also end. The diplomat's wife was young and Timoney would inevitably age out of his interest. Once that happened, she assumed he would be perfectly amenable to living separate lives.

Maybe Crete was right and it was a sad little life. But at least she would be *herself*. Not that mess of raw emotion and no spine to speak of that she became around Crete.

That had to be better. She was sure it was.

"Why are you smiling?" Crete asked her then.

And Timoney might regret what she was about to do. She knew she would. It had been bad enough to look upon the reality of Julian with Crete here in the room. It would be nothing short of a horror to truly let herself experience Crete once more only to walk down the little aisle in the chapel here tomorrow.

But she could handle regret.

Or anyway, she hoped she could.

Hadn't she already?

"Am I yours?" she asked him. "Truly?"

She saw something flare in his gaze, that brilliant shot of heat. And she could feel it inside her, far better than those other feelings of shame or horror.

Or this deep sadness she doubted would ever really leave her.

"You know you are," he said, his voice low. Thick. Hot.

And threaded through with a hint of deeply male satisfaction. Because, she knew, he thought he'd won.

For there was nothing Crete Asgar loved more than winning.

Especially not her.

But Timoney held out her arms anyway, because this was for her, not him. "Then prove it."

CHAPTER SIX

EVERYTHING INSIDE CRETE shifted into a long, low, simmering beat.

His chest. His temples.

Deep in his sex.

Timoney stood in the center of this curiously welcoming room bathed in buttery light. She was so beautiful it felt like a terrible ache to look upon her, and a greater ache that the man she thought she was going to marry had not seemed to notice.

He had looked at her as if she was a bauble, nothing more.

And Crete had no doubt that Julian intended to glut himself on her, but it was not the need in him it was in Crete.

It couldn't be, or he would not have left her here tonight.

There were a great many things that

Crete could have said on the topic of Julian Browning-Case, and surely one of them would have gotten through to her, but nothing as pointless as another man seemed to matter with Timoney's gaze on him.

That endless sea. Enduring. Beckoning. Blue enough to make a man believe in miracles.

He could not resist her. Then again, he did not wish to try.

Crete stalked past her outstretched arms, crossing to the door to make sure that it was locked. That it would admit no further visitors this night—and would not require that he debase himself any further by concealing himself behind the furniture as if he was taking part in some noxious theatrical production of a play he would dislike. When he turned back around, she had dropped her arms and had twisted around to watch him.

With a look on her face that suggested she thought he might have been on his way out.

The way he knew he probably should have been.

But Timoney had haunted him when he had never before believed in ghosts. She'd stayed with him even after he'd scrubbed his home of any stray trace of her presence. She had woken him in the night. She had chased him through his days and all over the world, never giving him a moment's peace.

He could remember, if vaguely, other women he'd been with for a time. He had always, eventually, felt a sense of great calm when away from them. That was usually how he knew that it was time to move on. When even sex could not give him a moment's peace. When leaving their side was far preferable to suffering their presence.

This normally did not take very long. Six weeks at the outside.

But everything with Timoney was inside out. Six weeks had come and gone and turned into six months, and he had still felt undone by her. Tonight he wasn't even touching her. He was gazing at her from across a room, having actually secreted himself behind some old pots so as not to distress her. All *she* was doing was looking at him with the expression he remembered best. The one that haunted him most.

Open and soft. Sweet and yielding.

It felt like peace.

And yet deep within that peace that only came when he was with her, and layered all around it, was this wanting that never seemed to fade.

When he had walked up to the house tonight, he had assured himself that all it would take was a glance in a window and he would feel the fool. That he would feel nothing when he saw her again. That he would melt off back into the night, taking his shameful obsession with her along with him when he left.

Alas, he had found her in the garden instead.

And *foolish* was not at all how he felt.

"Go back and sit on your little couch," he ordered her, in that tone he had always used when he intended to indulge his dark desires.

And like she always had, Timoney shivered. Visibly. He watched with a familiar surge of delight as goose bumps tracked down her neck and over her bare shoulders. His sex was like iron. His mouth watered.

He wanted to taste her more than he wanted his next breath. He would have happily traded it in.

When she did not move as instructed, he

only raised an eyebrow. And Timoney let out a rush of breath. Half a laugh, half a sigh.

A sweet music he had missed.

Then she turned, her dress rustling around her, as she set about obeying him.

"Pull up your skirts," he demanded, his voice darker than before. Hungrier. "I want to see you, Timoney."

She let out her little song again as she settled down onto the settee, the red cloak spread out around her like a scarlet frame.

And she kept her eyes on him as she pulled the skirt up, slowly, teasing them both.

He had taught her that, too.

Her legs were as perfect as he remembered them and he had to forcibly restrain himself from going over and getting his hands on her calves, her knees, her thighs. The hem of her gown skimmed along and then stopped at her thighs. She breathed in a deep, shaky breath.

Crete said nothing. He waited.

She took in another breath, then another, her gaze still locked to his.

He did not have to tell her to continue. And he did not wish to tell her. He wanted her to want him even a quarter as much as he wanted her. Even a sliver.

Timoney sighed a little, again, a soft surrender.

Then she pulled up the remainder of her skirt so that he could see the tiny scrap of fabric covering the V between her thighs.

"Bare yourself to me," he told her, hardly recognizing his own voice.

He could see the way she melted at that, but even if he had somehow missed it, she gave herself away. It was the way her fingers shook as she lifted up her hips and wrestled to pull her panties down, then tossed them aside. And she didn't wait for him to move his finger as he did, commanding her to take her place once more. She lounged back, spreading her legs wide, and holding her skirt up again.

The perfect picture of anticipation and abandon.

All his.

And because it made her shudder, he waited. Even though he was so hard he was surprised his trousers contained him, he waited.

Only when she sighed again, and there

was that little catch in the sound, did he move toward her at last.

Crete stalked over to that couch, refusing to admit that he felt something less than solid himself. Something less than sure. Holding her gaze, he sank down to his knees before her, placing himself squarely between her outspread legs.

He leaned in and the scent of her arousal rose between them, that raw, sweet honey.

Another thing that was only and ever his.

He hooked his arms around her thighs, hauling her toward him, then lifted her up before him.

And she melted for him, her body lush and supple and entirely his.

Possibly the only thing in this world that was always and ever his.

Crete could have spent a lifetime watching the way that flush moved over her skin. It reminded him that when she flushed, it went everywhere. Her nipples would become rosier, darker. The hotter she became, the pinker she would grow.

He could have spent still another lifetime cataloging the ways she burned bright, but he wanted her too much.

As he had always wanted her too much.

So he bent forward and put his mouth to the very core of her need.

And felt her as she shattered around him.

But he was only beginning.

Crete licked his way into her, holding her hips where he wanted them no matter how she bucked and moaned. He knew every contour of her. He knew what she liked and what she pretended not to like, but loved. He knew what set her to trembling and what made her sob.

He knew her.

And it was not enough to simply taste her. It was not enough to add one finger, then another, to the rhythm he set.

It was not enough to bring her to the edge then retreat, then throw her over again.

Again and again, just to make sure.

Just to remind them both.

None of it was enough. And he was drunk on her taste, on the sounds she made, on the way she brought her whole body into this. The way her heels drummed against his back and her fingers gripped his hair.

The way she rocked herself against him,

greedily. As if she, too, was as much a slave to these fires between them as he was.

Though he knew that couldn't be true.

For he knew that there could be no wanting deeper or wilder than his.

"Please," she cried out, arching up against him again. And then again. "Please, Crete. I need you inside me."

And it all felt preordained. She had always tasted too much like fate. As if he had been heading right here, to her, since before he'd even thought to take a drive this night.

He reached between them, pulling himself out. And there was no fumbling. There was no hesitation. He found his way to her entrance and found her molten.

Always molten hot. Always his.

And he thrust himself deep inside.

Timoney shattered again, this time on a silent scream that still managed to echo around within him.

Filling him. Scalding him.

Changing him, he thought.

He pulled her off her little couch and on top of him, so that she was straddling him where he knelt. Timoney came easily, gracefully. She wrapped her arms around his shoulders and took her time straightening, lifting her head from where it had fallen back.

And he could see the chaos in the blue of her eyes then. He could growl at the way she bit her lip.

"If you want me," he told her, in a low voice, "you must take me, Timoney."

He watched the way all that heat flashed in her eyes. He could feel inside him.

It had always been like this. One fire burning too bright in both of them, consuming everything. Taking them over. Making them ash and cinder, flame and fury.

A more beautiful immolation Crete could not imagine, then or now.

And then he found himself gritting his teeth as she began to move.

He had remembered every inch of her. Every touch committed to memory and trotted out to haunt him each night. Every moment of need and hunger made real since that first kiss. Since she'd lowered herself before him, tipped back her head, and stolen his breath.

Here, now, he could admit—if only to

himself—that he had thought of little else since she had quit his flat.

And still, somehow, it was as if he'd forgotten how bright she was, how intense. Or had diluted her effect on him, somehow, in the recollection.

It was the way she lifted herself, pulling away from his length and then dropping herself down again, making them both gasp a little at that slick, hot fit.

She was perfection, taking all of him and gripping him tight.

And she was his.

He had taught her this, this lush and lyrical dance. He had shown her all the different ways that they could light each other on fire. How to build these flames so that they danced high.

And how to ride them home, again and again.

He had taught her, and this seemed a celebration of that, of them. Her gaze locked to his. The way she rode him with all that artless determination made everything in him tighten as she rocked them closer and closer still.

Too good. Too right.

Too perfect to bear.

And then he could take it no more.

Crete tumbled her down to that soft rug beneath them, rolling her beneath him and placing his hands on either side of her head so he could change that rhythm. He went deeper, harder.

Her heels dug into the backs of his thighs as she met each thrust and everything then was fire.

That glorious fire, the delirious pounding, and when Timoney threw back her head to scream out her pleasure, he covered it with his own.

And only when she stopped shaking did he let go, thrusting jerkily within her until, finally, he surged over the edge at last—her name like a song inside him.

A song he took the time to sing to himself, for some time, while they both fought to find breath again.

It seemed to him a lifetime later when he could finally move. He took his time, rolling over again so that she was no longer beneath him, but instead splayed out across his chest.

And for another long while, another lifetime at least, she rested there, that soft weight Crete had not allowed himself to admit he missed.

More than missed.

"I'm glad we could settle this," he said. Eventually. And it was more than an olive branch. It felt...revealing. "We should head back to London now. We can send for your things in a day or so, when whatever commotion there might be tomorrow has died down."

And it was only when she did not make a happy, joyful sound, or nuzzle her face into the crook of his neck, that something cold moved through him.

"Timoney." His voice hardly sounded like his. "Everything is settled, is it not?"

She pulled away from him and sat up, smoothing her dress down as she went. Then she took a moment to push the masses of her silvery blond hair back.

And when her eyes found his again, they were steady.

Too steady.

It was as if the floor fell out from beneath him when he was lying there upon it.

"Things were not unsettled," she said,

as if she was choosing her words carefully. Very carefully, and yet her blue gaze did not waver. "On the contrary, they have felt very settled indeed for some time. Two months, I might even say."

Crete did up his trousers and then jack-knifed up. He resented that he had revealed himself at all, while she was apparently more than capable of *steady gazes* and bizarre statements. So bizarre, he assured himself, that it was no wonder they put his back up. "I do not understand you. Not a word you're saying."

Because she could not possibly mean what he thought she did. It was not possible, surely.

"You should return to London, Crete, but I will not be coming with you," she said softly. But directly. "I will be staying here. As I have told you all along, I'm getting married tomorrow."

"Don't be ridiculous." He could hardly get the words out, his jaw was so tight, and it seemed likely that it—that he—might shatter at any moment. "You have been rolling around on the floor with another man. *With me*, Timoney."

"And it is very likely that my husband-to-be might even now be availing himself of the woman he intended to roll around on the floor with in here." She lifted a shoulder, then dropped it, her gaze still offensively, outrageously calm on his. "It appears that I have found myself in a very open kind of arrangement."

"Have you been hit in the head?" he gritted out.

Her gaze cooled. "I have not."

"Because that is the only possible explanation," he continued, despite her reply. "For one thing, you cannot possibly imagine that the likes of Julian Browning-Case, so horrified at my parentage, would ever think that what's good for the gander is good for the goose, or whatever horrifying English phrase might fit."

"Whether it is or isn't, it is certainly no concern of yours."

He rubbed his hands over his head because what he wanted was to put them on her. And conduct another lesson. Maybe this time, it would take. "Timoney. Do you think I can't tell that you violently dislike that man? How can you possibly think you might marry him?"

But she only gazed back at him. Placidly. Even more placidly than before, as if the more he objected the more serene she became. "Because I have agreed to marry him, Crete." She waved her hand at him. "He gave me a ring and I agreed to wear it. More than wear it, I agreed to honor what it represents."

Crete was certain of two things then. One, that he needed to rip that diamond solitaire from her finger and toss it—and soon. And two, that she was taking some kind of perverse pleasure in this. In sitting there, still flushed from his touch, while she discussed her wedding as if it was something she wanted.

He could not believe it was something she wanted.

He did not believe it.

"Setting aside the fact that you looked at him with sheer horror," he managed to get out from between his teeth, "there remains the small issue of the fact that we did not use any protection whatsoever just now."

And he blinked when Timoney only smiled.

As if what he said was amusing, when he had never been less amused in his life. Since when did he forget protection? What madness did this woman stir up in him?

"How can this be?" she asked in mock amazement. "The pathologically overcautious Crete Asgar failing to use protection with a woman? Is this a typical lapse when you engage in one-night stands? Because for the six months we spent together, you never forgot it. Not even once."

"I never forget."

And at some point he was going to have to ask himself why, when that was an ironclad law he had followed for as long as he could recall, he hadn't thought about protection at all tonight. Not once.

But Timoney was only shrugging again, as if it was of no matter either way. "You heard what Julian said. He's prepared to accept any and all consequences of my liaison with you. What did you think he meant?"

Everything inside Crete went still. Like the moment before detonation.

Or the moment after. "I beg your pardon?"

"Surely you know that Julian has no heir," Timoney said, as if this was a casual little conversation they could have been having at the sort of dinner party he despised. "He doesn't even have a distant cousin to step up and take over someday. I think he's desperate. Or maybe he simply doesn't care. I don't know. But whether or not I'm pregnant is no impediment, as far as he's concerned."

She even waved a hand at that, as if dismissing the whole topic. As if dismissing *him*. And then she rose to her feet with that innate grace that Crete had always found nothing short of mesmerizing.

Even tonight, when he thought he might implode with the rage that stormed in him, she was spellbinding.

But he shook off the enchantment when she went to move past him, very much as if she was headed for the door. Yet another unacceptable choice on her part in a series of the same.

Crete shot to his feet, then reached out to take hold of her arm, turning her back around to face him.

She had the temerity to look shocked.

"The matter of your possible pregnancy may not signify to your groom," he gritted out at her, and was dimly surprised not to find himself shouting. "But I can assure you, Timoney, that it is of critical importance to me."

CHAPTER SEVEN

"THAT MAY BE SO," she managed to say with what she hoped sounded like a great calm. "But I'm afraid it doesn't matter."

He looked astonished, taken back, and possibly outraged at the notion that *she* dared tell *him* that his feelings were not of paramount importance across the Commonwealth, if not the whole of the planet. He also looked, unusually for him, faintly disheveled.

Because he was Crete, more stunning than any one man had the right to be, that his hair looked like he'd run his fingers through it only made him look better. However impossible that should have been.

And Timoney kept telling herself all these ridiculous stories, thinking that she could handle this, handle him. Yet the look of surprise on his face didn't thrill her the way it should have. It made her want to make it all better. To jump into his arms and race him back to London. Anything to make him happy—

But then, she'd already tried that.

She had to take solace in the fact that however he felt just now at the prospect of her wedding in the morning—and she could see how he felt, written all over his face— it was nothing compared with the way he'd made her feel that last night in London.

There was a part of her that was already racing to tell her exactly how much of a fool she'd been to allow this to happen. Because now it was all brand-new again. The feel of him, deep inside her body. His mouth moving over her tender flesh. The reality of him, so strong and hard and solid, pressing her down to the ground—

Just thinking about it made her tremble, everywhere, as if it was that close to the edge all over again.

Timoney tried her best to tamp it down, because the longer she stood here, looking at his rampant male splendor—his talk of taking her back to London with him ring-ing in her head, more temptation than any woman should have to bear—the more she had to face the facts. Chiefly that she already regretted this.

All of this.

Because she'd made a critical error here.

She had come alive again, with him. As if she had never been anything but a rush of brilliant color and raw sensation. Her two months of gray were over. She could *feel* again.

Timoney felt gloriously *alive* from her hair to her fingers to her toes and back. There was an electric current sparking within her once more, making her skin seem to glow. Her bones seemed to hum inside her limbs.

And every place he'd touched, inside and out, blazed still.

There was no undoing that. She wouldn't *want* to undo it.

She told herself that it had to be better to take this memory with her when she sank down into the swamp again. And if somehow she couldn't freeze herself solid again, well. Julian could do what he liked with her body. Timoney would go off in her head, come back here, and that, too, had to be better.

This way she wasn't losing anything. Heading off to London with him again, on the other hand, was a recipe for loss. Would it be six months again? Less? And when he was done with her again, when he had truly destroyed her—again—what would she do then?

Maybe she shouldn't have indulged herself with Crete, but she would have a long, safe marriage in which to consider the matter from all sides. She might not be happy, but she had chosen her path. It wasn't a seismic event. Like meeting Crete.

Like losing him.

She told herself the choosing was what mattered.

"I do not think that you are understanding me," Crete bit out. His grip on her upper arm felt like a band of steel. And that, too, felt like a gift.

Timoney would hoard it all up, these excruciating gifts like too-bright treasure. And her hoard was what would make the next few years fly by before Julian tired of her. As she knew he would.

She couldn't wait.

"I think I understand you perfectly." She

forced herself to meet his gaze again. "I just don't agree with you. I know that must be difficult for you, it being so rare."

Temper flashed over his face, and something in her seemed to roll over at that. Not in fear. Not in anxiety of any kind.

It was pure exhilaration.

Because the man Timoney had lived with in London had never let his veneer crack, even a little. There had never been a question that she might see beneath the masks he wore. The hard-edged businessman. The intense lover. The remote man.

This, too, was an unexpected gift.

"I am the bastard son of a man who could have taken care of me but did not." He bared his teeth at her. "You know this. You must also know that I would never, ever allow a child of mine to be raised apart from me."

Timoney couldn't let herself think about Crete as a child. It was too much. It had been bad enough to read those dry recitations of unfortunate facts in so many articles—but he had stood before her tonight and told her how little affection there was, how little kindness. She would dissolve where she stood if she let herself think about him as a small boy, surviving such coldness, and she couldn't afford that. He was a man who capitalized on the weaknesses of others, always. She admired that in him. It had made him who he was today, and she loved him.

But she couldn't allow him to use her own weakness for him against her.

"I'm sure you have nothing to worry about," she told him, though she was not sure of any such thing. Her body had always seemed to delight in its irregularity. She did begin to wonder, as she watched that dark incredulity move across his face again, what exactly she was playing at here. "I don't think it's the right time of the month."

"Somehow, this does not comfort me," he growled at her, as if he knew exactly how unreliable her body was. To say nothing of her claims.

"I'm sorry to hear that," she said in as British a manner as possible. Which was to say, she made it abundantly clear she was not, in fact, sorry. "Not everything is comforting. Some things hurt, Crete, and they keep right on hurting. Time doesn't change them. Space doesn't change them. Sooner or later, you either die or you learn to live with them."

And she felt his hand contract on her bicep as he took her meaning.

She hardly recognized him then, his face was so hard. His gaze so cold.

"Was this your plan all along, Timoney? Is this some kind of sick revenge?"

She pulled her arm out of his grasp then, too aware that he let her do it. It was disconcerting.

"Did you know you were coming here tonight?" He only glared back at her. "I will take that as a no. And no, I did not, in fact, plot out some kind of revenge. I had no idea you would turn up here."

Not this night. Not ever.

Not even though she'd spent two very long months wishing fervently that he would.

"But now that this has happened, you are happy enough to capitalize on it, is that it?" He shook his head in a kind of awe. Not a good kind. "I had no idea you were so ruthless."

That was rich, coming from him, but she suspected he wanted her to lose her temper.

One fire might lead to another, and then he would win. The way he always won.

"If you would like to sit down and answer more of my questions, fine." Timoney tried to look as if she was casually moving toward the door. Instead of what she was actually doing, which was making a break for it. "But if you're going to stare at me like that, as if you might at any moment begin to chew off pieces of me, I think I'll pass."

"You will not walk out that door, *Timonitsa mou.*"

The way he said that was alarming. She couldn't deny it. Every hair on her body seemed to stand at alert.

Especially because he didn't move.

As if he didn't *need* to move to cut her off. He was that sure of himself.

She told herself it was fear that raced through her, making her nipples harden into points and her core melt, but she knew better.

"I couldn't decide if I wanted to see you again or if I never wanted it," she told him when she reached the door. She put her hand on the latch but turned to face him because she felt she owed him this much.

It was more consideration than he'd shown her—and she also needed to convince him not to press her. Because her willpower to walk away from him and marry the man her uncle had picked for her was very flimsy indeed. "But I think that this has been good. It has eased something inside me, Crete. Though I doubt that was your intention, I'm thankful all the same."

"You are thankful," he repeated, his voice a dark and dangerous ribbon of sound that seemed to connect hard to all those places she was still trying to convince herself were fearful. And then set them all alight. "Oh, joyful day. You may be pregnant with my child. You insist that you will marry a man who disdains and disgusts you. But what can that matter when you are *thankful*."

Timoney felt as if her lungs were wrung out. She could only seem to take tiny little sips of air, and none of it seemed to get where it needed to go. Her hand ached, and she realized she was gripping the door latch far too hard.

But she didn't let go.

"Maybe he does disdain me," she replied,

her voice not quite as steady as she would have liked, because she might have been ignoring his other points, but that didn't mean the blows didn't land. "But at least he's honest and up-front about it. Which is more than I can say for you."

Crete reared back slightly, as if she'd struck him. "Try not to alter history of which I was a part, please. I was never anything but honest with you. I *am* nothing but honest, and to my detriment." His hard mouth twisted. "Ask anyone."

"You may be blunt and direct when it suits you, but that's not the same thing." She dropped her hand from the door and had the vague thought that she was making a strategic error, but she brushed it aside. And glared at him instead. "Are you ever honest with *yourself*?"

His eyes narrowed. And Timoney knew she shouldn't have let go of the latch. She should have left by now. She should have flung open the heavy old door, hurled herself out to the chilly hall, and then run all the way through this house until she could safely barricade herself in her bedchamber and count the hours until morning.

When you will do what? asked a sharp little voice inside her. *You will put on that dress you never liked but didn't wish to argue about? And then march down the aisle and shackle yourself to a man who thinks you're a whore?*

There was a sour taste in her mouth. She couldn't seem to stop flashing back to that particular look in Julian's eyes when he'd stood here before her, called her *my dear*, and called Crete a mongrel. She couldn't stop remembering the way his gaze had moved all over her, as if he was using his hands to find his way all over her body.

That was a preview. The voice inside her was certain. *And whatever made you think that because you've had so much good sex that you'll somehow be able to suffer through bad?*

And more, why had she imagined that she would be okay with that suffering? She didn't think Julian would hurt her. Meaning, she didn't think he would strike her. Yet it was suddenly occurring to her, much too late, that there was a vast gap between something that hurt—like a blow—and anything that was even remotely tolerable.

Sex had been a revelation. Having sex with Crete had altered everything. How she felt about her own body. What she did with it. How she viewed herself. She tried to imagine the same scene that had just occurred here on the floor of the conservatory, but with Julian rather than Crete—

Her mind balked.

Timoney hadn't been expecting revelations.

But she should have paid more attention to the cost of putting up with revulsion.

"Please," Crete said, still standing where she'd left him. Still seething. "Please do not lecture me on honesty. I am not certain that you have a handle on the meaning of the term as you prepare to walk into a wedding with another man, possibly pregnant with my child."

And this was not the time to think about what it might be like if she truly was—

It is not the time, she told herself sternly.

"Do you love me?" she asked him, her voice stark.

The way she had asked him once before. Fatefully.

First she had said those words he didn't want to hear, and then, when he had coldly explained to her the usual consequences for that, she'd asked him straight out.

Because she hadn't believed what was happening. And more, she already knew the answer. Or she thought she did. And she'd been so sure that if she simply asked it, he wouldn't lie. That he couldn't lie to her face.

Not like that. Not to her.

But he had.

Crete had looked straight at her, straight through her, as if she was a stranger. And with no hesitation, he had said no.

Just that. Just the one word. *No.*

Timoney would have preferred it if he'd slammed his fingers into her chest, actually torn out her poor heart, and crushed it beneath his foot. That he'd done it metaphorically had left her gasping for air. Why not do it in fact and let the pain of it kill her?

Then again, it had. She just hadn't had the pleasure of dying.

Now she was too alive for her own good and her wedding was at ten o'clock the next morning.

And she hadn't run off to nail herself

back into her coffin the way she should have when she'd had the chance.

Nor did she make a break for it now. She couldn't read the expression on his face any longer. It wasn't that cold, cruel mask from before. But there was nothing soft or loving about it, either.

Once again, she wished she hadn't asked.

"Do you love me?" he asked, and there was a dangerous edge to his voice then. "Does anything that you have done tonight feel like love to you, Timoney? Because I will tell you, it feels a great deal like love to me. That is not a recommendation."

After the story she'd gotten him to tell tonight, he could not have delivered a more devastating slap.

Somehow, she didn't let it knock her flat.

"You were right all along," she said quietly, when she could. "We are better off apart."

Then, finally, she turned to walk away from him the way she should have done in the garden, but her fingers no longer seemed to work. She fumbled desperately at the latch.

And when the world seemed to spin out

from her, tumbling around and around, she thought for a moment that she'd fallen.

It took her far too long to comprehend that he had come up behind her, spun her around, and tossed her over his shoulder.

"What are you doing?" she demanded.

She tried to brace herself against the wide wall of his back as he stalked through the conservatory. He swept up her cloak and draped it over her as she lay over him, then strode straight back out into the night.

The cold hit her hard, but mostly as a contrast to the heat of him beneath her. The cloak covered her and she was upside down, so there was no possibility that she could see where they were going—though she knew it was away from the house.

All she could do was hold on to him for dear life.

His strides seemed long. There was gravel underfoot, then grass.

She tried to roll off him, but his hand clamped down hard on her behind, holding her in place.

And, even now, making her melt all over him.

"Where are you taking me, Crete?" she made herself demand, because that felt like doing something. And surely she should *do* something.

His hand gripped her backside harder, the way he often did when he drove deep inside her. His shoulder was wide and sculpted beneath her belly, and she told herself the cloak was very warm and that was why she was suddenly too warm and given to squirm.

"Settle," he ordered her.

And he did not slow his pace at all.

"You must be mad," she threw at him. "You can't simply… What are you *doing*?"

"I should have thought that was obvious," he said, as he carried her off to the night. Walking tall and proud, as if it was his right, and gripping her backside as if he was claiming her. "As you cannot be trusted to make the right choices, Timoney, you are forcing me to make them for you."

Funnily enough, though she would have been delighted for him to make any choices for her that he wished a few months ago, she hated it tonight.

You mean you want *to hate it,* came that insinuating voice.

That made her something like desperate. "I beg your pardon. You have no right! Put me down this instant. *This instant.*"

She tried to throw herself to the side and he quelled it before she really even formed the thought. With a laugh. And the *quelling* made the core of her seem to hum.

"I cannot do that," he told her and if she wasn't mistaken, he sounded… at ease.

More at ease that she'd ever heard him before, in fact.

"What can you possibly be thinking?" she demanded, hardly able to hear her own voice over the clamor inside her, all of it spiraling around and around blooming into sheer desire between her legs.

"The time for thinking is over, little one," he told her, and if anything, his stride lengthened. "Now it is time for action."

"This is an abduction! You are *kidnapping* me!"

And this time, the hand on her backside smoothed over her curves, just enough to make every nerve inside her seem to dance itself awake.

Then shudder, like she was on the very edge of shattering.

"It is," Crete agreed, all dark male satisfaction. As if he knew. "You can thank me later."

CHAPTER EIGHT

THE LAST THING in the world Timoney wanted was to *thank* him.

Her pulse was a riot inside her. Her head was spinning, and not only because she was upside down. There was something buried inside her, something suppressed, that seemed to be storming its way out and she had no idea what might become of her then. She wanted to rip him apart with her fingers, to make him heed her cries—

Or that was what she told herself she wanted as he strode away from her uncle's house. Carrying her with him whether she wanted to go or not.

And she was terribly afraid that *thing* inside her, nearly free now, was a kind of triumph. Laced through with relief.

As if, despite what she might have said to

him in the conservatory, she reveled in the fact he'd made this choice.

Freeing her from Julian and her uncle and the choices she'd made while grayed out and dead within. Without her having to make them herself.

Maybe you should thank him after all, that voice needled her.

The world spun all around again and she found herself on her feet, but only briefly, as Crete set about strapping her into the passenger side of the gleaming Range Rover he'd left parked haphazardly near the estate's lower stables.

He slammed the door and strode around the front of the vehicle. And it was only when he swung in beside her that Timoney realized that she really should have used this opportunity to effect her escape.

Because surely if she had an opportunity to escape and she didn't take it, that was a choice. Wasn't it?

But instead of hurling herself out into the night and running for the questionable safety of the house, she'd been too busy contemplating the fact that Crete Asgar had actually turned up out of the blue. Had kissed her silly, then made her sob and scream on the floor of the only room in that house that had always felt safe. And had topped all that off by abducting her.

The night before her wedding.

On Christmas Eve.

And by the time it occurred to her that she really ought to try the door and see if she could outrun him, however unlikely, he was already turning the car around and heading away from her childhood home.

With what felt like a tremendous amount of finality.

Not that she was required to accept that, she told herself stoutly. *He* didn't get to decide.

"This is remarkably childish, Crete," she said as he headed down the winding drive. The December dark pressed in all sides and his headlights caught the remnants of the mist as it still collected in the hollows. Making herself sound reasonable and rational made her feel, if not in control, at least not as out of control as this situation *should* feel. "What do you think is going to happen now? Do you think removing me from the house will fix anything?"

"It will fix one, pressing matter," Crete replied, his eyes on the road ahead. "This is something you should know about me by now, Timoney. I always put out the biggest fire first."

But she knew that wasn't true, because the biggest fire of all still burned inside her. She was beginning to understand that it always would. No matter how much ice she piled on top of it, or how much gray she wrapped around herself. The flames were only ever banked, never extinguished.

"Sooner or later, whatever madness this is will pass," she said quietly, because thinking about the fires within wasn't helpful. "What gives you the right to wreck my life in the meantime? You had the opportunity to stay with me forever and you chose instead to have me tossed out of your flat. You don't want this. You don't like to be told no, that's all."

And she hoped he never knew what it cost her to sound so *serene* when she felt anything but.

"Surely it's time to set aside all this drama." But she could see that despite that tone he used, as if this was all the deepest silliness, his hands were like fists around the steering wheel. "You were not tossed out into the street like so much rubbish and I believe you know this well."

"Was I not? I don't recall you being there as your men hustled me along. I was given two hours."

He muttered something in Greek.

"Two hours," she said again, more distinctly. "And it wasn't that I needed more time than that to pack, Crete. It was that my lover, whose home I shared, told me that he never wanted to lay eyes on me again. I understand that this may come as news to you, but for most people that is the kind of blow that it takes some time to recover from."

The real truth, she knew, as she looked out at the narrow lane that he was driving along now—and much too quickly—hemmed in on either side by the hedges, was that she wasn't recovered. She wasn't sure recovery was possible.

Wasn't that how she'd ended up agreeing to marry Julian in the first place?

She glanced over at Crete. His face was set in harsh lines, his lips pressed together as if he was fighting off some of those emotions he would claim he didn't have.

And this was the trouble. She didn't like the feeling that she'd actually hurt him. She loved him. Whatever else happened, that didn't change. That he wouldn't admit something hurt him didn't mean it didn't. She knew that. Just as she knew that all hurting him did was hurt her. Maybe that was love, too.

Because no one had ever said that love meant happiness. Or that joy didn't have a price. She had thought the price she must pay was Julian, but in many ways this was worse.

For it was sometime after midnight, she saw on the car's dashboard. Technically Christmas, and that made a kind of sense, because this was a bittersweet sort of miracle. She had never thought she would see Crete again, and yet he had appeared like a dream. He had swept in like the mist, told her things about himself he never had before, and the way they'd come together could only and ever be love, as far as she was concerned.

Whether he would call it that or not.

She wanted to think that it was anxiety inside her, carrying on, ordering her to leap out of the car, demand that he turn around, do something to make it clear that she intended to marry in the morning.

But she knew better. She was trying to defend herself against the inevitability of the next time he would leave her. She *wanted* to believe in this. She *wanted* this Christmas miracle.

All while she knew that he believed in Christmas and miracles about as much as he believed in love.

For some time they drove in silence. Timoney could feel some tension leaving her the farther they traveled from the house. From Julian and her unpleasant future. And yet the farther they traveled from her childhood home, the closer they got to London and the more a different sort of tension grew in her.

Mile by mile.

"You," Crete said, almost softly, if that was a word that could be used for such a hard man, "are the only person I have ever met who has never treated me as if I was some kind of alien."

Such a soft yet sharp spear, thrust straight

through her heart. She folded her hands in her lap and stared down at them. "I don't think you're an alien. That would be convenient, wouldn't it?"

He let out a sound that she supposed was a laugh, though it seemed to curl around inside her like smoke and didn't help any with the weight of misery that seemed to sit on her then.

But she should not have felt miserable on behalf of her kidnapper. What was the matter with her? She ought to have felt miserable *because* she was being kidnapped, not because he might have tender feelings about it.

Something is very wrong with you, she told herself sternly.

Crete handled the country lanes easily, as if the towering hedges and slippery roads were nothing to him. As if the way the lanes wound this way and that was nothing short of soothing.

How she wished she could find a way to soothe herself—but she hadn't really managed that since she'd met him, had she? And she could hardly recall what had come before.

He made a low noise, as if he was coming to some kind of decision. She thought he sat a bit straighter behind the wheel. "You know my name is not actually Crete, do you not?"

"That is a wrinkle I did not see coming." Timoney frowned down at her interlaced fingers. "Though it would explain a lot if you had an evil twin. Did the bad version of you knock you over the head and lock you up somewhere? Is this the good version? I have a lot of follow-up questions."

He shot her a fulminating look, then returned his gaze to the winding lane.

"I was born with a proper Greek name," he told her, his voice a rasp across the darkness between them. "Adrastos Demetrios. My mother had many issues, there's no denying that. But she did not name her only son after an island."

And despite all the many articles that Timoney had ever read about him, she'd never encountered this little nugget of information. It seemed almost fantastical that he might have a name out there that no one had ever discovered. A secret name he was sharing only with her. Only now.

Something in her seemed to hum around

the syllables of that lost name. Adrastos Demetrios. Him but not him.

Another gift, that voice within whispered.

"Crete is traditionally a female name," he told her. "It is also the only place in Greece my father's wife had ever visited. So this is what she chose to call me."

Timoney turned in her seat, forgetting her own concerns as she studied his proud profile beside her. "Do you think she knew that it was a girl's name? Does she speak Greek?"

"She does not speak Greek, no." His mouth curved into that shape that was not a smile. "But my father does. I myself did not learn Greek until I was in school and could choose my own elective courses. As you can imagine, Greek was not encouraged in the father's house. And so it was my Greek teacher who first told me that my nickname was usually only used for girls. I think she expected me to be horrified."

"But you preferred to defy expectations," she whispered. "As ever."

"I legally changed my name to Crete when I was eighteen," he told her in that same dark rasp. As if it was painful to tell her this. "Because it was the only thing my father and his wife ever gave me. And though they meant it as a mockery, I'm certain, I chose to claim it as a prize."

Of course he did. This proud, remote man. Timoney had never wanted to reach out to him more. It actually hurt to keep her hands to herself.

And Crete was still speaking. "But more than that, it was a challenge. Let them laugh at a man with a woman's name. Let them amuse themselves at my expense. It would only make it all the sweeter when I crushed them." He let out that laugh again. "And, indeed, it did."

And any remaining doubts Timoney might have had that she was head over heels for this man, despite everything, faded away then. Because when he told her such harsh things, such sad reminders of the brutal place he'd come from, all she wanted to do was wrap herself around him and show him at least one moment of softness. At least one small bit of something better.

Tears pricked at the back of her eyes. "I'm sorry that even your name is a battlefield."

"Everything is a battlefield, Timoney."

His voice was low. Gravelly. "And I take a deep pleasure in winning these wars. It has been this way with everything and everyone, always. Until you."

Once again she felt winded, and she could feel the tears threatening to spill over. "That's not fair."

"Did you think this would be fair?" She only realized the car had slowed to a complete stop when he turned in his seat. His strong hand pulled her face around to his. "Love or war, it's all the same to me."

"You don't believe in love," she replied in a whisper, not jerking her chin from his grasp. Not fighting him.

"Maybe not, but I have always preferred war. It is simple. There are winners and losers. There is none of this mess."

"This is only as messy as you want to make it," she managed to say. "You could so easily have stayed away, Crete. You broke things off for a reason. You could have carried on as you have these past two months. What changed?"

"Nothing has changed." She thought she saw some kind of ghost in his gaze then. Or did she only wish she did? Either way he dropped his hand, though his gaze remained intent. "But you deserve better than Julian Browning-Case."

"Let's think about this rationally," she suggested, her gaze direct on his. "You carry me off like a caveman."

"Do cavemen drive Range Rovers?" His voice was arid. "I had not realized."

"Obviously there's a spark between us. I won't deny that. Let's say that I stay with you again. Or who knows? Find my way back to that listed house in Belgravia that you were so disdainful of earlier." She shook her head, still holding his gaze. "Sooner or later, it will be too much for you. Again. And by that time, perhaps, Julian will have moved on."

"Good," Crete growled.

Timoney sighed. "Julian isn't the point. If I don't show up at my own wedding tomorrow, my uncle will disown me."

"Is this a tragedy?" Crete demanded. "You'll excuse me if I do not weep. Whether your uncle disowns you or does not, all you will have to do is wait a few years for your trust to kick in. Is this not how it works to be an heiress?"

"You're talking about money, Crete. I'm talking about family."

"You don't even like your family." He sounded mystified.

"What does that have to do with anything? My aunt has her moments. And my cousins are perfectly unobjectionable." He had been honest with her about his name, so she swallowed, hard, and returned the favor. "And they are all I have left."

He shook his head, then turned his attention back to the lane before him. When the Range Rover began to move again, Timoney couldn't tell if she'd lost something or gained it.

"I know you don't understand family," she said, her gaze drawn back toward the way the headlights danced over the lane. The way the dark night held them fast in its grip, as if they were alone in all the world. Suspended here together in the quiet and the cold. "I don't expect you to. But until a few years ago, I would have told you I had the best family in the world. My parents loved me and I loved them in return. And I know that they would expect me to do whatever I can to maintain a relationship with my uncle and his family, no matter what."

"If your parents loved you at all, how could they possibly countenance your uncle's wish to sell you off to one of his cronies?" Crete made a dismissive noise. "A man who makes no secret of the fact that his only interest in you involves the marital bed. Was that what your parents wanted for you?"

Her parents seemed very far away tonight. But then, happily, so did any marital bed she might share with Julian. But what caught at her was that Crete had brought them up of his own accord. She couldn't recall him ever doing so before.

Much less speaking of love.

Her heart seemed to skip a few beats.

"My parents wanted me happy," she said quietly. She laced her fingers together again, because it was that or reach out to him and she didn't quite dare. "This is what I'm trying to make you understand, Crete. No matter what happens now, whether I am disowned or I simply go off with you for a time and come back to be married off to someone else, it's all the same, isn't it? I'm not happy. I'm not going to be happy. Because what I

want I can't have. You've already made that
abundantly clear."

"You don't know that."

But he drove faster, so that the dark and
misty night seemed a blur on the other side
of the windows.

"I do know that." She sighed. "I have no
intention of playing war games with you.
And you don't believe in love. Those are incompatible positions, Crete. You must know
that."

"Compatible or incompatible matter little
if you're carrying my child," he gritted out.

Her hands rested in her lap and she re-
sisted the urge to touch her belly. To imagine. "And if I'm not?"

"Then you will come to a place of grati-
tude, I have no doubt, for the act of service
this is," he said. With all his arrogance. "You
are not required to suffer that man's bed.
You are welcome."

Timoney kept her gaze on the dark blur
of hedge and distant sky. "But I won't be
happy, will I?"

Crete made a low noise. Disbelief. Temper. Some mix of both. "Are you suggest-

ing that you would be happier suffering with that pig?"

And Timoney blew out a ragged sort of breath. "Julian could never possibly break my heart. He could only harm me in small ways."

"I think you underestimate him."

"But you, Crete." She frowned at him. "You want to drag me off and pretend that we can go back to some version of what we were? At what cost? I've already tried loving you enough for both of us, and that didn't work. Why should this?"

She thought she could hear his teeth grind together, so hard was his jaw then.

"Maybe it would be better if we postpone these discussions until such a time as we know whether or not you are to be the mother of my child." He bit the words out. "I suspect that will answer any questions you might have."

"Putting aside the fact that you haven't thought to *ask* whether or not I wish to be a mother at all, much less of your child, what do you plan to do?" she demanded. "Will you fly me off to one of your solitary islands? Will you hide me away so that I dare not make you think about the things you'd rather avoid?"

"What will be the point in that?" he hurled at her. "When you would only haunt me either way?"

For a long while, as he drove through the darkness, Timoney sat with that.

And wished—oh, how she wished—that it could be enough.

Her cloak lay over her like a blanket and she pulled it tighter around her now, letting her eyes drift shut.

Once, it would have been enough to imagine she might haunt him. Once, knowing she affected him at all would have felt like a prize. Worth whatever she had to do to achieve it.

But she knew better now.

Timoney would never think it was enough until he admitted that he loved her the same way she loved him. Without limits. Without sense.

Wholly, desperately, and irreversibly.

Until then, she did not doubt that he wanted her. But she also knew he wouldn't keep her.

So she kept her eyes closed and she let

the rhythm of the wheels beneath her lull her into sleep.

Or into dreams, anyway, whether waking or not. Where she could pretend they might build a new life untainted by what had come before, or what she knew lay ahead.

Where she could pretend that love might finally be enough.

It was very early Christmas morning now, and maybe the true miracle was that she got this little space in between to imagine. To feel alive again. To remember the past without shutting down and to imagine the kind of future she knew they would never have.

To close her eyes in a speeding car and feel his presence all around her. To know, once more, the glory of his touch, and pretend for some little while that they could truly be together the way she'd always wanted.

It was a far better Christmas gift than she'd expected this year.

And Timoney would take it, for as long she could, before reality rained down upon her once again.

CHAPTER NINE

CRETE FOUND IT somewhat lowering that Timoney had actually fallen asleep beside him. He rather felt she should have been wide awake and on tenterhooks for the whole of the drive back into town, if only because *he* felt shot through with adrenaline.

As if he might never sleep again.

Still, when they arrived at his flat in London, he waved off the attendants in his garage and carried her into his private elevator himself.

And though her eyes fluttered open, he did not set her down until the lift delivered them into the stone foyer of his penthouse.

He opted not to examine the way he seemed to settle only when he carried her over his threshold, such as it was.

Then he found himself watching her as

she blinked the sleep out of her eyes. Without looking back at him, she crossed the foyer and walked deeper into the flat. She didn't stop to turn on any lights and for some reason, Crete did not do it as he followed her. He was too busy watching her as she went. She dragged the bright red cloak behind her as she moved to the great wall of windows that looked out over giddy London, laid out bright and gleaming before them.

He was growing tired of the way it hurt him to gaze upon her when she was not even looking at him in return. She stopped at the windows and raised the hand that wasn't clutching the cloak to her. He watched as she pressed her fingertips to the glass, let out a sigh, and only then turned to look at him over her shoulder.

"This must be the most beautiful view in all of London," she said quietly.

Though it felt far more portentous than a simple comment on the view.

And Crete felt that it was some kind of surrender on his part to walk to her, still shrouded in the darkness—or revealed by it—but it was as if his feet did as they liked.

Or as if he could not stay away, a voice in him suggested.

Then, either way, he stood with her at the glass.

"Of course it is the best view of London," he said. "Do you imagine I would tolerate anything less?"

He was looking at her as he said that, not at the view. And not because he was stunned by her beauty, though he was. But because she smiled then, and it was a sad, small curve of her lips that he could not say he liked at all.

"I'm sure it cost you a lot of money," Timoney said softly. She turned to look at him then, and there was a starkness in that sea blue gaze of hers that brought that same ache on again, harder this time. "But you don't ever look at it, do you?"

They were no longer in the car, so he did not have to pretend that the road held his attention. He reached over and hooked one hand around her neck, tugging her closer.

"Is this another metaphor, Timoney?" Crete kept his voice far softer than that ache in him, or the drumming noise of his own pulse. His own need. "I'm growing tired of all these games you wish to play with words. Both you and I know what is between us. It is a mystery to me why you would pretend otherwise, but I have solved it for you. It is already Christmas. You are here. And if I have to tie you to the bed to keep you from racing back to your wedding in a few hours, I will. Happily."

He was fairly certain that the reason she glanced away was to disguise the flash of heat he'd seen in her gaze. But he thought it proved how magnanimous he was that he did not tip her chin up. He did not force her to show what he knew was there.

Crete only waited.

As he waited for nothing and no one else.

"You don't have to tie me up, Crete."

He couldn't read the tone she used then. He couldn't parse it, and that was unusual. Crete had long prided himself on being able to see beneath the words people used. To see to the heart of things, where most people were usually hiding their true motivations.

But this woman confounded him. If he was honest, she always had.

"Are you sure?" he asked, silkily. Because he could think of any number of reasons that tying her up seemed like a fantastic idea, and not a single one of them had to do with the vile Julian.

Or that abomination of a wedding that he would not allow her to go through with.

The lights of the city outside seemed to play in her hair the way the moon had out in the countryside. And he found himself toying with the thick silk of it, without even meaning to. Without knowing what he was doing until he was curling it around his fingers and letting it spill through. While the hand that cradled the nape of her neck seemed to absorb nothing from her but heat.

Crete told himself that she was a provocation, that was all. And he was a man who had never allowed a provocation to go unanswered.

Why stop now?

"You have me here now," she said after a moment, with a certain directness that pricked at him. Perhaps because it did not whisper to him of tying her up in a bed and making them both wild. "You've made it clear that I'm not to leave. At least, not until you've made certain that my wedding is called off. I could try to run but, chances are, you would catch me. Or have your security team do it." She lifted her chin. "What now?"

His thumb moved on her nape, up and then down. Again, of its own accord. And he felt how she shivered, though he wouldn't have known it to look at her, so well did she hide what he could feel with his own flesh.

And Crete could not help but feel a powerful sense of loss, because once she would not have hidden her responses from him. Once, she had been all untutored enthusiasm, artless and sweet, running through his hands like sunshine.

He knew full well what had changed. And more, who had changed her.

But he concentrated on the heat instead. "Surely you and I can find a way to entertain ourselves, can we not?"

Again that smile, too sad for his tastes. "Is that what you want?"

Once more, Crete knew this was some kind of test. Like the stories she had demanded he tell her before. The answers she had needed him to give. Only this time, he had the distinct impression that this was not a test he could master.

And having her here again, in this space that he had always kept pristine, crisp, and utterly devoid of anything soft or even comfortable, brought it all back.

All of it, like a good blow to the head.

"You broke all the rules," he found himself saying, though he knew he should keep such things to himself. He had done his best to keep from saying such things for half a year while she'd lived here. He stood there, half in the dark and half lit up from London below, but all he could see was Timoney. "I do not indulge in public displays of passion in clubs. There's too much risk that it will all end up in the tabloids. But one look at you and it was as if I had no choice."

Her lips moved as if she meant to speak, but no sound came forth.

That was just as well, because Crete could feel a storm in him, gathering force. Driving rain, booming thunder.

Or maybe it was only his voice, telling her the things he had not told her the last night she'd been here. The things he'd had no intention of ever telling her.

The things he barely admitted to himself.

"There is an extensive vetting process,"

he told her as if he couldn't stop himself. He couldn't. "But I moved you in within the week. And the purpose of allowing a woman here is to make my life easier. So that I can concentrate on my work, give my all to my many business concerns, and have a woman here to fulfill my needs when and if I have the time. But you did not slot neatly into place here, Timoney. You…took up space."

This time her smile seemed something like rueful. "I suppose I did," she told him, her voice light but that intensity in her gaze. "But I had no choice. This flat is grotesque."

"I think you will find it is one of the most sought-after properties in London."

"It is grotesque," she said again, very distinctly, though her blue eyes gleamed. "Not only because of the fingerprints of too many mistresses before me, but because it might as well be a prison. Too much steel and concrete. Too many angles and cold expanses." She looked away as if she could see all the sharp corners and deliberately empty spaces without the lights on. "It's inhospitable to human life, Crete. I assume that's by design."

She was obliquely calling him an alien

now, and it was astonishing to him, how deeply he disliked it. The whole world could line up to tell him how unnatural he was. How little he fit in. He took that as encouragement. As a challenge.

But it was different when it was Timoney.

Still, she needed to understand. Somehow, he needed to explain all of this to her. What it had really been like, those months she'd lived here. How he had felt so unlike himself. Careening from one meeting to the next and yet hardly paying attention. Instead of feeling pleasantly set, all of his needs taken care of in their appropriate compartments, he had rushed home whenever he could. He had changed his schedule so many times his secretarial staff had been driven round the bend.

Crete had changed his whole life. Worse, he had been aware of it while he was doing it, aware of every step away from the man he had always been before her—but he hadn't been able to stop. He hadn't *wanted* to stop.

Still, he had been horrified that last night, when she'd told him that she loved him— when she'd cried it out in bed as if she couldn't keep it in another moment—that his first reaction had been a kind of mad thrill.

Because he could not seem to get enough of this woman. Of the total disregard with which she treated this ascetic sanctuary of his. How she left her clothes scattered about, so that he found buttery-soft scarves in improbable pastels lying about on his cold marble, his brutally minimalist steel. She was fluffy and bright, and seemed hell-bent on leaving her careless mark everywhere she went. She left dirty dishes by the sink. She plopped down mugs of tea wherever she happened to find herself, wholly and utterly heedless of any rings of moisture she left behind.

His housekeeping staff had been relieved when she'd gone.

But he had discovered quickly that without her, this luxurious, aspirational flat felt more to him like a tomb.

"I don't like mess," he said darkly now, to her claim that this place was designed to be inhospitable. "I don't like complications."

"And yet you were singing the praises of war earlier, weren't you?" she asked, lightly enough. Though her blue eyes seemed dark.

"I have yet to hear tell of any clean and uncomplicated wars, Crete."

"That very much depends on whether or not you are winning it, I think." His hands had moved now, without his knowledge. He was gripping her shoulders, holding her there before him, and he really could not have said if he meant to push her away or draw her closer.

He had never known.

"The trouble with you," he managed to grit out at her, though it seemed far harder than it should have, "is that you never fit here. You never slotted into place."

"I think I will take that as a compliment," she replied, as her chin inched upward. And the way her eyes flashed made him think he'd hit a nerve. "I was far too besotted with you to point out that no one particularly likes being *slotted into place* as mistress of the month. You do know how to make it all feel like a bit of an assembly line, don't you?"

"I do not recall you complaining about it."

She sighed. "I didn't, did I? But then, I knew I didn't fit in here, Crete. Much as I take that as a badge of honor, it only goes to show what I've been saying all night. Noth-

ing has changed, or will. I guarantee that
you will walk in here and find me far less
elegant than required. Too messy. Too determined to not slot nicely into the little box
you set out for the woman in your life. Eventually this will lead us right back to where
we found ourselves two months ago. Why
put ourselves through all that again?"

"I wanted to end things with you almost
from the start," he told her, as if the words
were being pulled out of him, backward.
"Every day I would come home to you, determined that I would draw a line under it.
Be done with it. Get my life back at last, so
that everything might run smoothly again.
That's how I like it, Timoney. Smooth, un-
challenging, predictable in every way."

Her eyes glittered. "I can see why you
stormed the family estate to abduct me away
from my own wedding, then."

"And yet I didn't do it," he continued on,
almost harshly. "Night after night, I didn't."
He shook his head, almost as if he had lost
this battle. When he did not lose. "Don't
you understand, Timoney? You broke all
the rules."

When all she did was present him with

that smile again—so bittersweet that it made him wonder if he'd had a heart all along, for what else could ache like that—he did not wait to hear what other arguments she might mount.

Because there was only one argument that had ever mattered. Only one argument that ever could.

He swept her up into his arms again and this time got his mouth on hers, and he kissed the ache away. Again and again.

Until it made a new one.

Crete carried her over to the low, long sofa that she had often complained was the enemy of comfort and sitting of any kind. He broke the kiss, his chest working as hard as if he'd gone for a run, but he refused to analyze why it was he was so desperate tonight when he had already won.

He had *won*, damn it.

And this time, when she smiled at him, it was filled with heat and need, passion and longing.

Crete felt it echo in him like relief.

He set himself to the critical task of removing her clothing, at last. Finally, he tossed that cloak aside, with all of its yards and yards of fabric that had concealed her from his view on the drive here. Then he tended to the dress she wore. It was a pretty enough garment, but there was nothing on this earth as pretty as what he uncovered.

Timoney George, naked before him.

The way he always remembered her. The way he always wanted her.

"You, too," she murmured, sounding impatient enough to make the fire in him blaze higher.

Her hands moved to his coat and then the two of them worked together, with what he was certain was the same sense of urgency, to strip him, too.

And when they were finally skin to skin, he tumbled her down on that couch she'd always hated and exulted in the feel of her. Here where she belonged, after the longest two months of his life.

Naked in his arms, at last.

Naked and wrapped all around him, and the singular joy of it was nearly enough to send him catapulting over that edge.

For another truth he had not told her was that the mistresses of the month had never been like this. None of them could hold a candle to her. He barely remembered them. Sex had always been a pleasant release, but Timoney was something else again.

It was the way her body fit to his, as if they were a set of interlocking parts that only made sense when they were together. It was her scent like honey. It was the way she smiled at him, hot and knowing, when he groaned. It was the way she traced her fingertips down his back, as if making certain he was okay. It was a thousand little things and only one thing, in the end.

It was *her*.

He wanted to take it slow, but it was impossible. There was a storm between them and Timoney liked nothing better than dancing in that rain.

While he liked nothing more than watching her dance them both into pieces.

They rolled, this way and that, until eventually she climbed astride him and took him deep into her body.

"Epitélous," he gritted out. *At last*.

The perfection of it. The slickness. That snug fit, so tight that everything else he was and all he felt seemed to expand in response.

She set their pace, taking him and teasing him in turn. Bringing them both to the edge, then retreating, until he couldn't tell if it was a game, or revenge, or some glorious combination of both.

And he couldn't care, not while he was inside her again.

Everything in him urged him to throw her over on her back and ride them both into oblivion.

But instead, Crete filled his hands with her round breasts. He pulled her face down to his to sample the bow of her mouth. He gripped her hips. And all the while he let her do as she would, drawing it out until it seemed the knife's edge they balanced on cut them both.

Deep.

And when he felt her go over, he watched it move through her. Timoney arched back, her hair all around her, beautiful beyond measure as she shook and shook and cried out his name to the steel beams far above.

Only when she slumped down against him, her open mouth to the crook of his neck, did Crete wrap his arms tighter around her and find his own, hard finish.

And it still wasn't enough. He was deep

inside her, her wildflower honey scent all around him, and it still wasn't nearly enough.

When he could move, sometime later, he lifted her up again and carried her across the length of the penthouse toward the master suite. He ran her bath, then joined her in it.

And he took her there, too, sitting there behind her. It was a sweet, shattering joining in all that heat.

But that, too, wasn't enough.

Later, after he'd finally taken her back to their bed and tied her to it—as much to make a point as because it was fun—he gathered her in his arms when they had both finally exploded, and held her there while she fell asleep.

It still didn't feel like enough, but he let her sleep. He let her burrow her face against his shoulder and murmur what sounded like his name in her sleep.

Such provocation, but all Crete did was stay awake.

He didn't dare take his eyes from her. There was some part of him that worried that this was some rare dream. That he had never left the flat tonight. That Christmas morning was coming up fast and she would wake in that cursed old house, pull on a white dress, and marry that horrid old toad.

He stayed awake because he wanted this to be real, not a dream.

Because he was beginning to understand that when it came to Timoney, he would never, ever get enough.

CHAPTER TEN

WHEN TIMONEY WOKE, she knew exactly where she was.

She had dreamed that she was back here so many times in the past two months, curled up happily just like this. The heft of his pillows. The astounding softness of his sheets. The lightweight clasp and warmth of the duvet. The scent of him surrounding her, sinking into her, making her feel soft and molten and ready before she was even fully awake.

At first she didn't open her eyes. She simply let herself drift in the particular embrace of this bed she knew so well.

When she did open her eyes, it was to find that she wasn't dreaming, this time. She really was in Crete's wide platform bed, the way she had been so many times before. The way she'd been so certain she never would be again. It made her shake a little to find herself here. It made her feel a bit too raw.

She pulled in a steadying breath as she sat up, shoving her hair back. On the other side of the three walls of glass around her, it was still dark. Timoney pulled one of the almost scandalously luxurious blankets with her as she went, more so she could keep feeling it against her bare skin than any particular sense of modesty.

The room itself was as she remembered it. Profoundly stark, featuring only the imposing, masculine bed in deep gray linens against the single gray interior wall. There was concrete everywhere with steel beams above and London on three sides, right there on the other side of the private terrace.

When she had lived here, she had liked to tell herself that it was a kind of urban tree house, that was all. Made of concrete and steel instead of wood, but the same, really. It had helped her feel less dizzy, perched so high above the Thames and the streets below.

But that had only helped so much. It was

still too far off the ground, too cold and impersonal, for her liking. She'd made the best of things, because what else was there to do? This was where Crete lived, so she had made her home here, too, however uneasily. She would have camped out in an actual tree house in a field if it had meant that she got to live with him, sleep with him, make love with him at will. She would have put up with any indignity.

Timoney told herself she ought to be embarrassed by how easily she'd surrendered herself to this dour concrete world of his. But even as she thought it, she was shaking her head. Because she hadn't really surrendered, had she? She had lived here, but she hadn't paid the slightest bit of attention to his rules, stated and unstated alike.

Because she had been so sure that she would win him over. That she would introduce a little color into his life, not by actually coloring over his dark grays and steels and concretes, but by virtue of becoming that color herself. Timoney had danced naked on his excruciatingly hard sofas until he smiled, however unwillingly. She had painted the wall in his study and him, too, when he'd glared, affronted, at her makeshift mural. She had cooked elaborate, messy meals in his pristine kitchen, using up every pot and getting the ingredients everywhere. She had laughed when he'd scowled. She had imagined that she was the antidote to the rest of his hard, busy life.

In truth, she had taken pride in that role.

It had never occurred to her that it could ever end between them. That he would end it.

The overconfidence of virgins, he had said once. In a manner that had made it clear that it was not a compliment,

But Timoney had only laughed at him, then had crawled onto his lap in the back of the car they'd been in. *Entirely too overconfident,* she had agreed. *Shall I show you?*

She swung her legs over the side of the bed now, still too raw. And remembering everything too keenly. Even the height of the platform the wide bed sat on seemed to poke at her, casting her back into far too many memories.

It's like a throne for sleep, she had said once.

A throne for something, Crete had replied. *But not sleep, I think.*

And then he had demonstrated what it was for. Repeatedly.

Even thinking about the kinds of demonstrations he liked best made her shiver a little. She saw the strips of fabric he'd used earlier in a heap on the floor beside the bed and smiled. That was the thing about Crete. Whatever he dedicated himself to, he gave it his all.

Always.

She padded around the bare, imposing wall that served as a headboard, but Crete was nowhere to be found in the rest of the expansive suite. Something in her shifted uneasily as she looked into one room, then the next, but didn't find him.

Though she stood a moment in his study, staring at the mural she'd made him that she'd been sure he would have had re-painted within twenty-four hours of her departure. It shocked her that it was still there, all the bright and garish colors she'd slapped all over the wall opposite his steel-and-glass desk.

Timoney didn't know how to feel about the fact the mural was still there. But it was nothing short of alarming that he wasn't at his desk. As far as she knew, the study was the only place he went in this sprawling flat of his when he wasn't making use of his bed.

And she found that she was…apprehensive as she went out into the rest of the penthouse. Had it already happened? Had he already changed his mind?

Just because she'd known he would, that didn't make her prepared for it now that it had happened. And so soon.

Was he even now readying his vehicle to whisk her back to Oxfordshire and hand her off to Julian?

Funny, wasn't it, that she found that prospect nothing short of unbearable now.

Crete was nowhere to be found in the flat. But as she stood naked in the center of the great room, Timoney discovered that the relief she felt had only intensified after a very few hours of sleep. And it brought with it some clarity.

She did not want to marry Julian.

She did not want to experiment with his brand of marriage, much less what he would expect of her physically. Even if he tired of her in six months, that was too long. As she already knew from her time with Crete, six months could be a lifetime.

And imagining a lifetime with Julian made her stomach hurt.

She almost laughed at herself then, though it really wasn't funny. Even while she and Crete had still been in the conservatory, she'd been telling herself all kinds of stories. First and foremost, that it had been possible to imagine she could suffer through Julian's attentions when she'd still felt so dead inside. And then she'd tried to convince herself that she would somehow carry the much fresher memory of Crete with her, perhaps so she could retreat into her head while giving Julian what he wanted.

But now, only a few hours later, she couldn't understand how she'd managed to convince herself that such suffering was possible.

Maybe, something in her suggested, there in the unlit penthouse with only the relentless London gleam outside to light her way, *all you really wanted was to punish yourself.*

For giving so much of herself to man of steel and concrete, thinking that a few bright colors on a wall could make him love her.

For falling in love with him when he was only having sex with her.

For letting down her lost parents by failing at happiness, and love, and hope. Again.

For that overconfidence when she should have known better. Shouldn't she have known better?

Because surely she should have learned something from losing them so suddenly. From everything that had changed afterward, irrevocably. How had she managed to throw herself at Crete the way she had, so appallingly *certain* that she could make the both of them happy, when she knew better? Happiness could be snatched away at any time. At any moment, like it or not. Life was all about the lie that it might last, but she knew better.

Timoney had known better—but her grief hadn't been enough to save her.

Not from Crete, but from herself and her own overweening confidence. Her abominable belief that her own feelings, her own heart, could make things end well.

When she knew they didn't.

She turned back around and headed for the bedroom again, thinking vaguely that she might as well shower, then get dressed again. Then she could wait for whatever next bombshell Crete would reappear to drop on her.

There would certainly be time enough for considering the ways she'd been punishing herself then. In the great stretch of *after* that would follow this one, last night. Where she could find a way to deal with how raw she felt that did not involve upsetting weddings, surely.

She vowed that she would make a point of it.

But when she made it back into the bedroom that was never truly any kind of a tree house no matter how dearly she'd wanted to convince herself, because it was really much more of a prison cell, she saw what she hadn't before.

Crete, who had not left her. At least not yet.

He stood outside at the railing at the edge of his terrace, wearing only a pair of low-slung black trousers, as if it wasn't December.

Then again, this wasn't just any grubby old flat and he wasn't risking hypothermia for the sake of showing off his sculpted torso to the uncaring night. The section of the terrace just outside the master bedroom was fitted with heated floors, making it far more inviting to make use of the sauna and hot tub nestled there, high enough above the city that there was no possibility anyone could be spying on what any resident here got up to.

Timoney dragged the soft blanket off the bed and wrapped it around herself, then pushed her way out through the glass doors.

And she knew the precise moment Crete became aware that she had come outside to join him. She saw him tense, ever so slightly, and got to watch the muscles play all up and down the chiseled length of his back as she drew closer, the heated concrete warm enough beneath her feet to make the cold air feel like a caress against her exposed face.

It still moved in her like wonder that she had touched every part of what surely was the finest back in England. Worthy of being cast in bronze, at the very least. She felt that same old heat that never left her bloom hot within, making her thighs seem to whisper sensually as she moved. And the core of her pulse with need, as if it was new.

She came up beside him, but he did not glance at her. He kept that brooding gaze of his focused out on the city at his feet.

"You're really not good at this kidnapping thing, are you?" she asked lightly as the night air made her ears cold and her hair fly about. "I was left to my own devices entirely. I could have made a break for it while you stood out here, none the wiser."

She didn't expect uproarious laughter. Not from Crete. But he seemed extra grim, she thought, especially after everything that had come before this night.

"Do you wish to escape?" he asked, far too darkly for her tastes. "Have you woken with second thoughts? And a renewed determination to sacrifice yourself at the altar of two old men's greed?"

That was a little too close to what she'd been thinking on her own. "And if I have?"

He pushed back from the rail but still gripped it. And when she glanced down at his hands, she saw that his knuckles had gone nearly white.

"Then I will be forced to disappoint you,

Timoney. You will not be marrying Julian today. Or any day."

She could have told him how much her thinking on that had changed, but she didn't. She could have explained, talked about punishing herself, or even asked him why he hadn't erased the evidence of her terrible mural, but she didn't do any of that, either. Because he was straightening, then turning to face her, and the look on his face was… terrible.

It looked almost like passion, drawing him tight and taut.

But passion she could handle. Or she knew she would survive it, in one form or another, anyway.

Somehow, she knew it would not be as simple as that.

Timoney braced herself, for surely the look on his face meant that a cutting verbal blow was to follow. From a distance, she almost felt philosophical. How would he make it worse? He would have to, she assumed, to really make this hurt. He had devastated her last time. How would he—how could he— make that seem like child's play?

She had been so unprepared before. She'd

been so in love that it had never occurred to her that anything could come between them. It was almost cringeworthy now to look back at how naive she'd been. She'd fallen so deeply and surpassingly in love with him. She had cheerfully offered up every part of her, heart and body and soul, with no hesitation and no catch.

The fact that it *could* end—that *he* could end it—had never crossed her mind.

Luckily, she was far more worldly and prepared now. He had seen to it personally.

So Timoney lifted her head proudly, tipped up her chin to take whatever he might toss her way, and told herself that come what may, she would be fine.

One way or another, she would be *fine*.

Eventually, something in her whispered.

"We should get married," Crete said, as if there was glass in his mouth.

As if the words shattered as he said them and were cutting into him as he spoke.

Timoney only gazed back at him while the December night slapped at her exposed face, certain she hadn't heard that correctly. "What did you say?"

If anything, he looked more in pain. Anguished, even.

"We will marry," he said, his voice like gravel. "That will put an end to all of this, I hope. If you must be trapped, Timoney, you might as well be trapped with me, don't you think?"

She was glad that she had thought to bring the blanket, not only to save herself from the chill of this Christmas predawn morning, since it seemed her feet had gone numb beneath her and she might never be warm again. But because it gave her something to grip as she tried to process what he was saying to her. Tried to make it make some kind of sense.

And came up with nothing, though her hands began to ache from the force of her clenched fists.

"Crete…" she began, though she hardly knew what to say.

Especially because, as reluctant and grim as he sounded—as clearly unwilling as he was—there was a part of her that didn't care about any of that.

Because she remembered that girl, only two months ago, who had loved him so wildly and so deeply that she had simply assumed it would end in marriage. Sooner or later. Because how else could it end? She had known, with a bone-deep conviction, that forever was the only possible destination for them.

And there was still some part of that girl inside her tonight, because she wanted to simply throw herself at him. To ignore all the warning signs and the red flags, his grimness and the things she'd learned these last months, and simply…say yes.

Because no small part of her wanted nothing more, ever, than to take this man however he came to her.

Just so long as he came to her.

But while it had been only two months since her last, awful night in this flat, it had been an instructive two months.

"This is what you want, is it not?" And he sounded even bleaker than before. "I will marry you. Then there will be no more concerns about appeasing your uncle. Whether he disowns you or does not will be a matter of little practical import if we are wed. Whatever olive branches you wish to extend to the rest of his family you can do without having to worry about his approval."

It seemed to her as if London was spinning all around them, but she focused on him.

"Why would you do this?" Her voice sounded far rougher than she wanted it to. It gave too much away.

"It is only a few years until you come into your own fortune," he muttered, seemingly to himself.

"It is five years, in fact." She tried to swallow, but her throat was dry. "Five years is a very long time, Crete."

He seemed to turn to stone before her. "Nonetheless, marrying me will solve all your problems."

"I must still be asleep," Timoney said after a moment, searching his face and seeing nothing but granite and reluctance. "And I don't mind telling you, I've had this dream before. Many times. So I can tell you what I've often told myself when I've woken up to find your proposals little more than wishful thinking." She had to clear her throat then. "You don't actually want to marry me. And martyrdom doesn't suit you at all."

He let out a bark of laughter. "I am many things, but I have never been a martyr."

"Then why pretend you want to marry me?" The words felt wrenched from her.

Because she still wished she could…just say yes. Come what may.

His gaze grew darker than the night around them. "If that is what it will take, then that is what I will do."

Timoney gazed at him for a long while, until it seemed to her that she was only hurting herself that way. She turned her head then, taking in the sweet stretch of sleepy London, here in the dark before dawn on this Christmas Day that she had expected to go very, very differently.

And later, maybe, she would explore all the ways that this moment, in many ways, had hurt her more than anything that had gone before. But she needed to make it through, first.

Somehow, she had to survive this, too.

She sighed, though she wanted to sob. She stood straighter, when she wanted nothing more than to collapse into a ball on the ground.

"I appreciate the offer," Timoney made

herself say, though everything in her was a riot of a sharp, bright anguish. She wanted nothing more than to snatch her words back. Then answer differently. Just jump straight in, because surely, whatever happened, it would be worth it—she would have him in some way and that had to be better than not having him. But instead, she made herself keep going. She made herself do the hard thing. "But no."

He gazed down at her, a thunderous expression taking over from the bleakness. And that was better. More familiar, anyway. Because at least she recognized his arrogance.

"No?" he repeated, incredulous.

"No," Timoney said, more firmly. "I am not going to marry you, Crete."

The incredulity on his face became a scowl. "Why the hell not?"

And she couldn't keep track of the things she felt any longer. Because she felt too many things at once. Still the urge to sob, holding all the smashed broken pieces of her heart in her hands. But also, possibly, she felt the urge to laugh, too.

Because someday, surely, she would find

all of this funny. This man, who no one said *no* to, clearly. The look of imperious astonishment on his face, as if he'd never heard the word before.

She supposed it was possible he hadn't. Not really. Not since he was a child.

"We've never talked about Christmas," she said quietly, her gaze still on the city streets far, far below. But she made herself turn then, to look at him. "I'm going to guess by the singular lack of anything even remotely festive in this apartment of yours that you don't care for the holiday."

"I don't like holidays." His scowl deepened. "Particularly Christmas. The only thing worse than festivities are forced festivities. Perhaps you haven't noticed, Timoney, but the whole of England appears to slide into a minced pie stupor come fall, and little sense can be had from anyone until the new year. It is tiresome."

She found herself smiling again. Not happily, perhaps, but still. It was a smile. "It's very easy to get caught up in all the trappings. Minced pies, for example. Festive decorations, the race for perfect gifts, carols and fizzy drinks."

"Do you require that I present you with gifts?" he demanded. "Perhaps you have forgotten who I am. Have an island. A fortune or two, if you wish it. It means nothing to me."

Timoney shook her head and held the blanket closer. "It's not about the trappings. I know you don't understand Christmas, and maybe you never will. When my parents were alive it was my favorite day of the year. And not because we exchanged gifts, but because we were all together and everything was as it should be. A fire in the grate. Happy songs in the air. Terrible jumpers and a proper home-cooked meal. Just us. Just *love*, Crete. All the rest we could take or leave, as long as there was love."

His jaw seemed more like steel than the railing he gripped. "Simply name the meal you wish to be served and I will make it happen."

As she supposed she should have known he would. He could buy her anything she claimed she wanted. He could send a text and buy out restaurants all over this city, even forcing them to open for him today. If he wished, he could do almost anything.

Almost. "I thought that with Julian it wouldn't matter, because I already felt so numb, so what was little more self-harm? But you saved me from that. And I'm grateful, I am. But now I understand far better than I ever could have before that Christmas, marriage, it's all the same, really." She shook her head, trying to keep her emotions at bay, because she couldn't quite believe that she was doing this. "It's not about what you can *buy*, Crete. It's about what you *feel*."

"Timoney—" he began, looking thunderous again.

"It's light and it's hope, Crete." Her voice cracked. That was how urgent this felt to her. "And you think those things are the enemy."

"I do not. Necessarily."

"You do." She didn't address the *necessarily*. She didn't have to. She could see it written all over his face, all his rationalizations and qualifications, and none of that mattered as much as what she was about to say. "You do, Crete. And because you do, that means eventually—inevitably—you'll think I'm the enemy, too."

And Timoney realized that some part of her was waiting for him to refute what she'd said…when he didn't.

It was amazing, truly, how much an already broken heart could still continue to break.

"You will say yes," he thundered at her. "You will, Timoney."

And she knew what he would do even as he did it. He swept her into his arms again, and carried her inside.

It was only back in the heat of his flat that she noticed how cold she'd become. When he laid her out on the bed and followed her down, and the passion she knew she would hold close to her heart for the rest of her life exploded anew.

He warmed her the way he always did.

"You will," he promised her as he drove deep inside her, making them both groan.

"I won't," she replied, wrapping herself around him, putting her mouth to his ear. "But I will tell you goodbye, Crete. Every way I can."

And that was what she did.

With every part of her body, her heart, her

soul. Again and again, in all the dark before dawn they had left. Because she knew that once the sun rose, reality would reassert itself, as little as she might want it to.

But first it was this. First there was them.

First there was a small taste of forever that would have to last her in place of the real thing.

CHAPTER ELEVEN

CRETE DID NOT SLEEP.

He could not.

He stayed wide awake long after Timoney finally drifted off. She lay beside him, curled into him, her breathing deep and even. Sometimes she murmured wordless chants in her sleep, as if she was dreaming of giving long speeches. But all it took to settle her was to hold her close again.

Sometimes when he held her, she smiled with such pure, sleepy happiness that it pierced him straight through.

But no matter how he tried, he couldn't seem to sleep himself.

He left her reluctantly and swung out of the bed, noticing the first stirring of dawn in the sky outside his windows. As good a time as any to remind himself who he was, he told himself sternly as he moved back into the flat. He took a quick shower—cold—to reset. Then he threw on a pair of trousers and retraced the steps he'd taken a seeming lifetime ago when he'd decided to take that drive.

It had started in his study. He'd been catching up on the never-ending fire hose of work projects that required his input or a critical decision to proceed. And privately, he could admit that he was no longer quite as driven as he'd been once.

Though that felt like a betrayal of the determined eighteen-year-old he'd been long ago, who had thrown himself so completely into his work that he hadn't known where one ended and the other began. It was all him. It was only him.

Until Timoney.

He took his usual seat at his desk but didn't turn his attention to the stacks of papers before him, the blinking light on his answerphone, or the many messages he'd been ignoring all night long. He didn't even crack open his laptop.

Instead, Crete found himself staring at the wall opposite him and the ridiculous mural that Timoney had painted there. It had been blank for years. Deliberately empty space before him to keep him from being distracted.

He'd flown home from a conference in Berlin that day and hadn't gone into his office the way he normally would. Instead he'd raced home to discover her here. She hadn't seemed the least bit put off by his reaction to the bold, bright colors she'd painted—or to her presence in what was meant to be his sanctuary.

You really need to think about brightening yourself up, she'd told him with that great, unearned authority of hers that had baffled him from the start. And bewitched him, against his will. *Maybe make that an action item in one of your meetings, Crete.*

You need to think about boundaries, he had growled back.

And the smile she'd given him had been pure wickedness. *Maybe you should teach me some,* she'd invited him.

He had. Oh, he had.

But what he hadn't done was take that mural down. Not even after she'd gone. And even now he couldn't seem to come up with a good reason why not. His staff had offered, repeatedly, and he'd simply waved them off.

And now he sat in his chair once again and stared at all the haphazard splashes of color, tossed this way and that as if she'd simply flung paint at the wall to see what might happen. Brilliant blues. Screaming reds. Sunshiny, buttery, happy yellows.

The bloody thing was an eyesore.

Crete found himself on his feet. He left his study and walked through the flat, turning on the lights as he went, though the sky outside was brightening and light was beginning to come in all the walls of windows.

It was one of the most sought-after spaces in London. It was the finest view available. That was why Crete had bought this place. But for the first time, he noticed what Timoney had been saying from the moment he'd brought her here. That it really was…institutional.

You are the richest man on earth, or close enough, she had said not long after moving in. *You can have anything you want, in triplicate. Why on earth have you chosen to live in this…prison?*

Her words seemed to chase him as he moved through his rooms. Rooms upon rooms, all of them empty, because the point was having them, not filling them. Concrete and steel in the place of furnishings, because he told himself he liked clean lines and no clutter, the better to focus. Selected works of art chosen not because they were pleasing to him, but because they were worth vast fortunes.

He didn't even look at them.

What Crete looked at—what he studied, day and night—was that mural Timoney had painted for him that would likely offend and horrify his art dealer.

And it all made sense to him now.

The problem wasn't the mural. He'd tried to convince himself, in these last few weeks, that he kept it on that wall to remind himself of the defacement he'd allowed. To make sure he never forgot how wholly he had abandoned himself for a woman.

Making him more like the father he had always detested than he found at all excusable.

But now it was clear.

Everything he did, everything he was, was a prison. This was a cell of many fine rooms and he little more than a prisoner of his own making.

He found himself standing stock-still in the center of the nearly empty great room his expensive decorator had assured him was the height of sophistication. Not that he'd cared either way. His only interest in sophisticated people and their elegant pursuits was in showing up to prove that anyone could buy the things they all held so dear.

That they could hate him all they liked, but he never went anywhere.

But he'd missed the fact that he'd made that…literally true.

This flat was a prison. His life was a prison. When he'd clapped eyes on Timoney outside that club, she'd been like a key in a lock he'd stopped noticing was there ages ago. She'd wedged open the door. And instead of finding his way out, he'd slammed the heavy bars into place again.

The word *prison* kept echoing in his head.

And it seemed perfect that he'd come to this realization while it was not quite daylight outside.

Because she had spoken of hope and light. It seemed he needed her to do that so that he could finally see all the bars around him. The ones he'd put there. Day after day, year after year. Building this cell and leaving himself here to rot.

Hope and light was a silly, soft sort of notion he would have laughed at, before her. He would have slept soundly, tossed her out the first time she'd left her things about, charged right on into the next project and the next and the next...

But now he understood.

Now he understood everything, and it was as if he was ripped wide open from the inside out, so that too much understanding poured into him, battering him.

Changing him.

Letting him know that truly, he had been changed for good long ago.

Outside a club, at a party he hadn't wanted to attend, when he'd caught eyes with a girl who'd looked like a moonlight over the Mediterranean.

She'd smiled at him and he'd never been the same.

And maybe it was finally time he stopped fighting that.

Crete was finally ready when she woke again. It was light outside and coming up on ten o'clock, when she was meant to walk down an aisle out in the country and hand herself off to a man who would stamp out every last trace of light in her as if it had never been.

Whatever happened here, at least he had saved her from that darkness. He could take some solace in that, surely, for there was no one alive who deserved to wilt away in the darkness less than Timoney.

He knew the moment she sat up in his bed, so attuned was he to the sounds in this prison of his. *Or perhaps it's the fact you've lived here for years but have never truly moved in. If you had bothered to put rugs on the floor there would be nothing to hear.*

Crete accepted that was true, little as he liked it.

He waited out in the great room, listening to the sounds she made as she moved around in the back of the flat. He heard the shower go on, then off some while later, leaving him with too many images of her lush body in hot water and slick with soap.

But today was not about his libido.

Or so he kept telling himself, until his jaw was so tight he was surprised it didn't snap.

Sometime later she appeared, her blue eyes still sleepy and her hair wet, buttoning up an old shirt of his she must have liberated from his wardrobe as she walked. Along with what he thought were a pair of his boxer briefs. Her favorite uniform, as he recalled.

As always, his heart seemed to swell at the sight of her. But today he didn't pretend that wasn't happening. He simply stood there and watched her come toward him, letting his heart do what it would.

And maybe because she was still half-asleep, her eyes lit up when she saw him the way they always had, before.

The way, he promised himself, they would again.

Because he watched the way she pulled herself back as she remembered why she was here today, and he'd done that. Crete knew he had. He watched the shutters close down her expressive face and knew that he was the only one responsible.

And God knew he couldn't bear the thought that any part of her should be dimmed.

But he didn't have too long to contemplate

that because her eyes widened again in the next moment, as she came to a stop beside him and took in what he'd done.

"What… What is this?" she stammered.

He found himself scowling.

"Christmas." His voice was gruff. "Obviously."

Timoney moved past him, farther into the room. And he turned to look, too, wondering what she saw when she looked at his handiwork. This work of the few hours he'd had.

Because she had talked of Christmas, so he had ordered one up, paid dearly for it, and had transformed this room she'd had always hated.

Now it bristled with evergreen trees, all of them festooned with lights. So many lights it made the cavernous room feel warm and enchanted. It made this prison of his look the way he felt when he gazed at her.

The way he felt right now.

And it didn't feel at all natural to simply… let himself feel. Not to hide. Not to divert. Not to pretend it wasn't happening.

"Crete."

But the way she said his name was barely

more than a whisper, laced through with wonder. Or what he hoped was wonder.

And he was ready when she turned around.

He stood there before her and though he had dressed at some point during his Christmas morning rush, he felt as if he had never been more naked.

"I do not want you to think that I am trying to impress you with what I can buy, *Timonitsa mou*," he said stiffly. "That is not what this is."

She looked almost stricken. Her hands moved as if she was reaching toward him, but she dropped them back to her sides. "Crete. I…"

But she trailed off when he shook his head. And he had the distinct impression that he looked more severe than necessary… Then again, he didn't have it in him to make this easy.

He didn't do easy.

There were some who had been born with that sort of charm, but he was not one of them. Everything he'd ever gotten in this life had come from hard work. Day after day, year after year, when it yielded great results and, more important, when it didn't. He wasn't afraid of work.

In many ways it was the only love he had ever known.

But it was a cold love. A harsh love. It could give him a splendid prison and a life filled with only the finest things, but it couldn't make him as happy as a splash of yellow across a wall. It couldn't look at him with eyes brighter than the sky.

And it wasn't what he wanted any longer.

Crete had never faced a harder task— or a steeper mountain to climb, in his life of bounding over them like they weren't there—than this one.

"Your wedding was due to begin five minutes ago," he said, sounding darker than necessary. "I am surprised that no one has rung you, demanding to know your whereabouts."

She seemed to consider that. "Happy Christmas to you, too." And she didn't precisely smile then. But there was the hint of that wickedness he'd known about her. "And I imagine they have rung me repeatedly and searched the whole of the estate by now.

What will all the abducting, I didn't have time to leave a note. Or fetch my mobile."

He studied her, telling himself to do this correctly. "Do you wish to contact them now and explain?"

Her chest rose and fell, hard, as if she was having trouble keeping her breath even. "I… do not." When he only waited, she sighed. "I suspect my absence will speak for itself. I imagine that Julian will think it's because I saw him in the middle of a dalliance last night, but that can't be helped."

"I can return you to your uncle's house, if you wish it," Crete made himself say. No matter how bitter the words tasted on his tongue.

She stood a little straighter then. "I do not wish it."

"Are you certain?"

"This is the first day of the rest of my life, Crete," she said softly. "There are a great many things I wanted to do with my life before I loved, then lost, then allowed myself to get talked into a wedding I never wanted. Before my parents died. Maybe I want to do some of them. All of them."

He nodded at Timoney's hands, and the ring she wore.

"You can start by taking that ring off." And he was not an uncertain man. As far as he was concerned, all he need do was think it and it became law, but this was Timoney. He cleared his throat, then forced out the unfamiliar plea. "Please."

It was distinctly unfamiliar, and uncomfortable, to admit to himself that he had absolutely no idea what she would do next.

Timoney blinked. Then she looked down at her own hand as if it surprised her to find it was connected to her. She frowned for a moment, then she wrenched the diamond off her finger. Then, holding his gaze again, she simply…tossed it.

Crete had never heard a finer music than the faint clatter the ring made as it hit the floor, then skidded out of view beneath one of the trees.

"Did that feel good?" he asked.

And she smiled at him. That beautiful smile that had knocked his whole world askew the first time he'd seen it. And every time since.

"As a matter of fact," she said. "It really did."

So while she was still smiling, brighter than all the lights on these trees he'd put up just for her, Crete did something he had never done before in the whole of his life.

He sank to his knees before her. Then he reached into his pocket and pulled out the ring he had acquired by waking up London's foremost jeweler at the crack of dawn. On Christmas. And then making it worth the man's while to come here, bearing boxes lined with velvet, so that Crete might make his selection.

And no matter what happened next, it would be worth every last penny the man had wrung out of him for that service—simply for the look on Timoney's face as Crete knelt there before her.

"I wanted to give you Christmas because I want to give you everything," he told her. "I want you to do every one of those great many things that you dream about."

"Crete." His name was a whisper. "What are you…?"

But he couldn't think too much more about what he was doing or he wouldn't do it. He would retreat back behind his bars and live a life of cold steel and concrete. Darker and darker all the time. He might end up there still.

First, though, he would try to walk out of his cell, once and for all, and reach for the things he'd always told himself he didn't want or need, because they slowed everyone else down. Love. Companionship. The vulnerability of it all. The longing and the need and the perfect happiness of lying next to her in the dark, close and whole.

He had stopped holding out his hands when he was still a child. But hadn't his childhood taken enough from him? Two families. His name. His heart.

Crete held out his hands now.

And for the first time in as long as he could recall it, he let himself hope.

"I want to give you light," he told her, as if he was carving the words he spoke into the stone beneath them. "And I want, more than anything, to give you love. And all the hope you can handle. But I think you know how little I know of each. Light is one thing."

He couldn't look away from her. He didn't want to look away from her.

She stood before him, her hands over her mouth as if she couldn't believe what she was seeing. Wet hair and bare feet. Her face scrubbed clean. His boxer briefs.

Crete had never beheld more beauty. It filled him up. It coursed through his veins.

It made him believe.

"All I know of light or hope is you, Timoney."

He had never knelt before because it had always seemed like surrender to him, but he knew better now. He had never been more powerful than when he dared to do this. To hand over his heart to this woman, knowing full well that she could hurt him more, and more critically, than he had ever been hurt before. She could destroy him. But he did this anyway. "And any belief I might have in love, is you."

Crete held out the ring he had chosen, because it had reminded him of her. It was a precious moonstone, large and almost iridescent, surrounded by enough diamonds to sparkle the way she did.

"Are you...?" Her hands were still over mouth, so her words were muffled, but her eyes were bright. "Is that...?"

"I want to marry you, as I said last night," he told her. "But not to wait out your uncle or your money or whatever other nonsense I might have spouted. That was me trying to hide. But I do not wish to hide any longer, Timoney. I… I love you."

He thought she whispered his name.

But he pushed on, his voice growing rougher with each word, because he had said it. And now he needed to say the rest. "You make me imagine that I am a man. Not a mystery or a monster or an alien creature set down amongst these humans I cannot understand. With you I am only a man, flesh and blood and capable of loving you as you deserve." He shook his head as if to clear it. "I don't know if I ever will, but I know that I will start by setting aside all this anger, all this pain I have long tried to pretend was only fuel to me. I will let it go, Timoney. This I promise."

This time she said his name. He heard it perfectly.

"Because, *Timonitsa mou*, you are light and you are hope, and there is nothing I cannot do when I put my mind to it. Only look around you." He kept holding the ring out between them, his gaze locked to hers as if he would never look away again. "If you give me the chance, I will spend my life trying to be the man you make me when I am with you. I will learn to be as you are, with the courage of a hundred fearless lions, prepared to fight for even as dark and twisted a heart as mine. And so sure, despite everything, that you would win. How could this not inspire me? I will dedicate myself to making you as happy as you can be, and making up for what I have put you through. I will leave my past where it belongs. Because what I want is the future. Every possible future. With you. And I promise you that I will love you, as best as I can, until I draw my final breath."

He realized his heart was pounding. His head felt alarmingly light. "If…" He cleared his throat. He dared to hope. "If you will have me."

And then he waited, his whole existence in the balance. In her hands.

For a long moment Timoney only looked at him. A great deal as if she was seeing a ghost.

And then his heart dropped, for her beautiful eyes filled with tears.

And he thought, *There it is, then.*

For there could be no arguing. There was no point in temper. It was one thing to bluster and carry on. He was good at that.

But it was another to offer his heart, unadorned, and have that be rejected.

Crete understood in that moment not only how it was that people died of broken hearts, but how easy it would be to succumb. Because how was he to go on with a heart that no longer beat?

But then, before he could even think about lowering his arms, Timoney's beautiful face broke wide open into that life-altering smile of hers.

Wider now. Brighter.

Then she was rushing toward him, hurtling herself into his arms.

Crete caught her, bearing her down with him onto the hard floor and turning so he could cushion her. She was so busy pressing kisses all over his face, his neck, that it took him a beat, then another, to hear what she was saying with every touch of her lips to whatever part of him she could reach.

"Yes," she whispered, fervent and fierce and sure. So very *sure*. "Yes, I will marry you. Yes, I will love you. Yes, Crete. *Yes*."

And so it was there, lying on the floor surrounded by his first Christmas ever and all the bars of his prison busted wide open, that he slid that ring onto her finger.

Then started his most important project yet: loving her forever.

Which, it turned out, he was as good at as he was everything else he touched.

Because Timoney was light. She was hope made real. He was grateful for her every day of his life.

But he was still Crete Asgar.

CHAPTER TWELVE

A YEAR LATER, to the day, Timoney George walked down the stairs of the house in Belgravia she and Crete had picked out together to marry the man who waited for her there at the bottom, in a grand hall thick with brightly lit Christmas trees.

She had never felt more alive.

"My love," Crete said, his dark eyes intent on her as she descended the sweeping steps toward him. "You are a vision."

And her smile was so wide she was afraid it might actually break her wide open. But maybe she wouldn't mind too much if it did.

This had been the best year of her life.

It had started in that cold, cavernous flat that he'd somehow filled with Christmas and it had only gotten better. Day by day.

Her uncle was still not speaking to her, but

despite what her parents might have counseled had they been here, Timoney could not bring herself to consider his silence a loss. She had used Julian's behavior with the diplomat's wife as an excuse and Uncle Oliver had only sneered and told her to grow up.

Timoney felt that it had been a sign of how grown up she really was that she had not engaged with him any further.

Julian had been even more difficult. He had blustered and tried to bully her when she'd called him. Not because she'd wished to talk to him, but because she did not intend to hide from the choice she'd made. She had not called so he could soundly abuse her for the better part of a quarter.

Which he had done at top volume until Crete, who had been holding her in his lap while she sifted through the wreckage of the life she'd walked away from, jumped in. He suggested that Julian seek redress for whatever damages he felt he had faced through Oliver, as Oliver was the one who had set the wedding into motion in the first place.

And if you do not care for that solution, Crete had continued with a cool menace, cutting through Julian's outrage that easily, *I can assure you, this mongrel would be only too happy to let loose the full power of my legal team upon you.*

Timoney had never heard from Julian again. Happily.

When she and Crete had gone back to fetch her things after New Year's, her uncle had quitted the house in protest. But her aunt had met her at the door. Hermione had insisted that Timoney and Crete stay for tea with her daughters, and had even, in an act of defiance the likes of which Timoney had never seen before, eaten a petit four.

Her daughters had been wide-eyed. Timoney had been filled with hope—for all of them.

Things had only gotten better from there.

She and Crete had looked for a place to live that felt like a home, and had settled on a house not far from the listed house she'd lived in before she'd met him, that he had once mocked.

And because they built what they had now around joy, anything was possible.

Anything was possible and nothing could take it away.

Every day that passed, the deeper it got. The better it got.

Crete learned how to delegate, turning over the parts of his businesses that no longer thrilled him to his fleets of underlings, all of them desperate to prove themselves. Timoney learned that when a person had been given everything on a platter, as Crete had once accused her, the best thing to do to live a meaningful life was turn around and start offering platters to those who might need them. She set up the George Foundation in her parents' honor, and by that fall, was ready to throw her first ball.

Where she and Crete had danced together, in public, for the first time.

She could still recall every moment of that waltz. His ring on her finger and his hand in the small of her back. His dark blue gaze fierce and proud.

And that crook in his lips that was only and ever hers.

That smile that would have told her how much he loved her—even if he hadn't spent a good part of each day making sure she knew exactly how much.

A favor she took great pleasure in returning.

"Are you ready, *kardia mou*?" asked the man who waited for her today, resplendent in a dark suit and unrecognizable from the Crete she had known before.

Because this Crete smiled. This Crete was transfigured by love. By joy.

By all the hope and light they could handle.

"More than ready," she told him, taking his hand.

And he led her into the room where their officiant waited.

A room filled with the life they'd built together. Art that made her heart hurt when she looked at it. Comfortable places to sit, to lie, to explore each other in every possible way. Rugs on their floors and happy plants.

The house they lived in together was filled with books. With laughter.

With enough love to light up the whole of London.

And often did, by Timoney's reckoning.

Today they stood in the middle of a beautiful Christmas and gave themselves to each other in a new way.

And after they said their vows—after Crete kissed her and murmured marvelously possessive words against her lips that she took pleasure in returning—he swung her up into his arms and looked down at her, beaming.

Not an alien at all, this glorious man of hers. But her husband now.

And more than that, too.

But she would save her little secret for later. After they moved from this private moment that they'd wanted to be only theirs into the banquet hall where their friends waited. Her friends, that was, and Crete's half siblings, because this had been a year of new beginnings in every possible way.

Because joy made even the unimaginable possible, day in and day out.

They would feast and they would laugh. They would dance as husband and wife. They would toast their new life and ring out those Christmas bells.

And then later Timoney would share with him that there was yet another new life they could celebrate in six months' time.

"Hope and light," Crete said to her, like another vow, as he carried her into the hall to the sound of cheers within.

"Hope and light," she replied. "Forever."

But every part of her was bright and awake and alive now, and ever would be. Because Timoney knew that for them, forever was just the beginning.

* * * * *

If you were wrapped up in the drama of The Bride He Stole for Christmas *make sure you don't miss these other stories by Caitlin Crews!*

His Scandalous Christmas Princess
Chosen for His Desert Throne
The Secret That Can't Be Hidden
Her Deal with the Greek Devil
The Sicilian's Forgotten Wife

Available now!